Praise for Carol Stephenson

"An emotionally compelling story
dealing with the pain of child abuse and manipulation,
and the healing power of love."
—*RT Book Reviews* on *Nora's Pride*

"[It] will grab you by the throat and
provide many pulse-pounding moments of excitement."
—*CK²S Kwips and Kritiques* on *Shadow Lines*

"This one packs a powerful punch [and] a
sweetly poignant ending. I strongly recommend
this book for all lovers of romantic suspense."
—Reviewers International Organization
on *Shadow Lines*

Praise for Maggie Price

"Maggie Price is a premier novelist of any genre."
—*Cataromance.com* on *Banking on Hope*

"Maggie Price is a master at drawing suspense lovers
into her spellbinding series."
—*Singletitles.com* on *The Ransom*

"The cleverly developed plot
is filled with unexpected twists and turns."
—*RT Book Reviews* on *The Cradle Will Fall*

"Smack in the middle of a tense procedural mystery,
Ms. Price demonstrates why she is the best
at writing about cops and romance!"
—*WritersUnlimited.com* on *Hidden Agenda*

CAROL STEPHENSON

Award-winning author Carol Stephenson lives in southeast Florida with her beloved shih tzu. She's an attorney by day and author by night. She's best known for her emotionally drawn, hard-driving romances. In her free time this sports fan indulges in travel, photography and debating NASCAR races by the water cooler. You can keep up with Carol and her books on her Web site at www.carolstephenson.com.

MAGGIE PRICE

Before embarking on a writing career, Maggie Price took a walk on the wild side and began associating with people who carry guns. Fortunately they were cops, and Maggie's career as a crime analyst with the Oklahoma City Police Department has given her the been-there-done-that background needed to write true-to-life police procedural romances. Those stories of gripping suspense and sizzling romance have won numerous accolades, including a nomination for the coveted RITA® Award. Maggie is also a recipient of a Golden Heart Award, a Career Achievement Award from *RT Book Reviews,* a National Readers' Choice Award and a Booksellers' Best Award, all in series romantic suspense.

NASCAR®

What He Didn't Say

Carol Stephenson  Maggie Price

HARLEQUIN®

TORONTO • NEW YORK • LONDON
AMSTERDAM • PARIS • SYDNEY • HAMBURG
STOCKHOLM • ATHENS • TOKYO • MILAN • MADRID
PRAGUE • WARSAW • BUDAPEST • AUCKLAND

ISBN-13: 978-0-373-18537-5

WHAT HE DIDN'T SAY

Copyright © 2010 by Harlequin Books S.A.

The publisher acknowledges the copyright holders of the individual works as follows:

Recycling programs for this product may not exist in your area.

CHASING THE TRUTH
Copyright © 2010 by Harlequin Books S.A.
Carol Stephenson is acknowledged as the author of "Chasing the Truth."

CORNERED
Copyright © 2010 by Harlequin Books S.A.
Maggie Price is acknowledged as the author of "Cornered."

NASCAR® and the NASCAR Library Collection® are registered trademarks of the National Association for Stock Car Auto Racing, Inc.

This edition published by arrangement with Harlequin Books S.A.

For questions and comments about the quality of this book please contact us at Customer_eCare@Harlequin.ca

® and TM are trademarks of the publisher. Trademarks indicated with ® are registered in the United States Patent and Trademark Office, the Canadian Trade Marks Office and in other countries.

www.eHarlequin.com

Printed in U.S.A.

CONTENTS

An excerpt from Hilton Branch's prison journal...

A man takes pride in his sons.

Pride goeth before a fall, isn't that the old saying? I've been thinking a lot about my twins lately. It's nearly time for the exhibition race, and I remember so well the first time I took Bart and Will, my twins, to it when they were kids.

They both became drivers in the big show, the NASCAR Sprint Cup Series. I'll never forget the first time I watched the two of them in their cars with Branch Mutual Trust big as life on the hoods, my boys right up there with the best drivers in the world.

They're both set to compete in another exhibition race this year—a man's chest could burst open with the pride of it. They'll battle hardest with each other—they always did. They're each other's best friend, but there's no one either would rather beat than the other. Their mother couldn't take how competitive they are, so way back when they first started in go-karts, Maeve set up a system—she takes turns rooting for them, wearing their team colors and all that. It's the way a mother ought to be, I guess, but she's led a sheltered life. She doesn't understand that it's a jungle out there, but I'm damn glad they do.

My sons and I, we had good times. We *did.* They used to think their old dad was ten feet tall.

Bad things happened, but I never meant to let them down. I don't imagine that I'll ever get the chance to say so, though. None of my grown children has seen fit to pay me a visit in this jail or even send me a card. I didn't expect any better of my youngest, Sawyer—I never really understood that boy.

But my twins, I did everything for them. For my princess Penny, too—created the opportunity for my beautiful girl to have that modeling career she always wanted. She appeared on the cover of many a fashion magazine, even did a swimsuit issue one year. I was so proud of all of them, but now not a one of them wants anything to do with their father, and damned if it doesn't hurt. Maeve would probably say it's my just deserts, but there were good times.

There *were*.

Sure, I grabbed for life, always. Wanted to scale the highest mountain, had to reach for the biggest piece of the pie. When you grow up dirt poor you have appetites, and for a long time, I satisfied all of them: the mansion, the vacation homes, the expensive cars and planes and boats. I took good care of a lot of people—too many, it turns out.

In the end, everything fell apart. If my children would give me a chance, I'd explain.

Maeve and I made a sort of peace before I went to trial. I told her I was sorry, and I am. She drops me a line now and then, most recently to include a picture of Penny's little girl and to tell me that Will and his wife, Zoe, are the parents of twin babies now, a boy and a girl. I can't get over the idea that my Will has gone and gotten married, and to Zoe, of all people, even after what I did to get that girl out of his life so he could focus on racing. Because of me, Will missed the first ten years of their son Sam's life, another black mark he'll hold against me.

I'd like to talk to him now. See if being a father changes his opinion of me.

It gets real lonely in here.

But in a few days, I can at least watch my boys race.

Chasing the Truth

Carol Stephenson

In honor of cancer survivors, their supporters,
and those who soldier on to fight the brave battle.

CHAPTER ONE

HE'D BEEN LYING to himself, Holt Forrester conceded as he dodged three men chest bumping in the graveled parking area by the New River Gorge. Minutes earlier the trio had parachuted together to a flawless bull's-eye landing. "Congratulations," Holt called out without stopping.

Had he really thought he could handle the crush of people in attendance today? Managing his investments based on cold hard data was one thing. Directing a tired mother with a wailing toddler to a Port-a-Potty was totally outside his comfort zone. Still…

Pausing, he glanced up to the gleaming span of bridge eight hundred and seventy-six feet above. Another jumper yelled a battle cry as he somersaulted off the platform. Moments later a white parachute popped open against the blue sky. Holt smiled.

Unbelievable. He'd actually done it. He'd pulled off the fundraising event for breast cancer without a hitch. All the months of convincing everyone in the West Virginia government from the governor to the Division of Highways to allow this special day of BASE—bridge, antennae, spans or earth—jumping had paid off.

The adrenaline buzz of his own jump still pumped through Holt along with pride and satisfaction.

He had known those adventurers who thrilled to parachute free falls wouldn't be able to resist the lure of a legal jump off the second-highest bridge in the United States. All in the name of a good cause, the Amanda Forrester Jump for Cancer.

An event to honor his mother. He'd been only twelve when she had lost her battle with breast cancer, but the memories of her efforts to maintain a normal life for him and his father despite her pain remained seared in his soul.

The latest jumper splashed into the river. Volunteers gunned motorized inflatable rafts and raced toward the man to pluck him from the water.

Holt released a sigh of relief. So far the event had gone without any major injury to any of the participants. Only a cut here, a bruise there.

The only other thing that would make this day perfect would be to meet the woman with the smoky-warm voice who had called him from Double S Racing. Emma-Lee Dalton.

He looked around for his assistant. Ted would know if she had registered. He might not be able to find her in this crowd, but surely she would be at the auction following the jumps. Double S Racing had been more than generous in its donation of NASCAR racing memorabilia, and Holt suspected that the very enthusiastic Ms. Dalton was largely responsible. He wanted the opportunity to thank her in person...and see if the woman matched the voice, he admitted.

"Hey, Holt!" Stan Preston hurried toward him. "Did you see all the NASCAR bumper stickers in the lot?"

"Yes, I did."

Stan huffed to a stop. The older, heavier-set man wore carefully creased khakis, a blue oxford-collared shirt and navy windbreaker. He pulled a handkerchief from his pants pocket and mopped his brow.

"Wasn't I right about NASCAR? The fan loyalty is incredible. Once I got the word out that the organization had donated items for the auction, the fans hotfooted over here."

"You were right, Stan." Not only had Holt been impressed

with the man's contacts at NASCAR, but he'd been amazed by the surge of registrations after the auction announcement.

Stan beamed. "You understand now why a NASCAR sponsorship would be a smart business move for your launch of the new software line?"

"I'd be a fool not to." Holt had met the insurance magnate when Stan had consulted with him about developing computer programs. When Stan had gotten it in his head that he wanted to start his own NASCAR team, Holt had been one of the first he'd hit up for sponsorships. A sponsorship seemed to be good business, but Stan's new team might not be a good fit.

Holt never jumped into a deal, which is how he'd made his millions. He needed more data before he made his decision. He hadn't even divulged to Stan the true nature of his latest computer venture. Although the Internet was alive with rumors, he was keeping the game under wraps for now as much as possible.

"Holt." Stan looked concerned. "When I was checking out the auction display, I noticed a number of items from Double S Racing. The owner, Gil Sizemore, isn't wooing you as a sponsor, is he?"

No point mentioning to Stan that he inexplicably had found himself flirting with the Double S's representative. Hearing her bubbling laughter over the phone had caused him to hit the Delete key at an inopportune moment on a report he'd been reviewing at the time.

Holt shrugged. "My P.R. person mentioned that the individual racing teams might donate if I contacted them personally, so I did. Business is business, no matter whether it's for charity or not. You should know that better than anyone, Stan."

The insurance magnate hadn't exactly amassed all his agencies by being an emotional pushover.

Stan relaxed only fractionally. "I'm still trying to get you a few pit passes to the upcoming races. Those passes are harder to come by than a rate increase."

Holt glanced up at the bridge. With her pink jumpsuit fluttering in the breeze, a woman stood on the edge of the platform and appeared to be talking with the volunteers. Why wasn't she jumping? He glanced at his watch.

Only thirty minutes left in the permitted time, and he had at least that number of people waiting for their turn. "Excuse me, Stan."

Walking toward the riverbank, he spotted his personal assistant helping another jumper. "Ted, I need your radio."

"Sure thing, Holt." The young man hurried over and handed it to him. He pointed out the solid line of bystanders lining the bridge above.

"Can you believe all the people who came to watch? What a show they got today! The vendors are selling food and souvenirs like hotcakes. This is going to rake in a ton of money."

"I couldn't have pulled this off without your help, Ted."

The assistant flushed at the praise, but one of the volunteers called for him from the control center they had set up by the river. He hurried off.

Holt looked up again. That woman in her pink jumpsuit still stood there. Was she frozen with fear?

He activated the walkie-talkie. "Davey, what's the holdup? If that woman's gotten cold feet, get her out of there."

Not everyone could stand at the end of the sixteen-foot-long ledge and take that step off into emptiness.

"Not cold feet, Holt. She's just going on and on about how pretty the gorge is and what a momentous occasion this is."

He rolled his eyes. "Tell her to gawk later."

"10-4."

Moments later, the woman directed a smart salute at him. Then she lowered both arms to her sides. This was it. That minute when you prepare mentally for the leap and say a prayer.

Then he felt it, the breeze stirring.

"Holt!" Ted ran toward him. "The storm we've been watching is now coming faster."

Holt raised the receiver. "Davey, weather's moving in. Stop the jumpers…"

Too late. The woman raised her arms and executed a perfect swan dive off the platform.

He handed off the radio to Ted and raced to the water's edge.

One second. Alone in the air she would experience perfect quietude, not the howling wind when one jumps out of a plane.

Two seconds. She would be picking up speed with wind whistling through her clothes and the ground rushing toward her.

Three seconds. Pull the chute.

Too long, too long. She would hit the ground hard.

Relief flooded him as the purple-and-red parachute snapped open, making a colorful splash against the darkening sky. He watched as she guided it. She was going for a bull's-eye landing in the taped-off spot behind him.

He'd made it himself, so he understood the desire to make a controlled landing, one where you bested the elements.

The wind picked up and the chute turned. He recognized by her movements that the woman was going with the change and would land in the river where the rafts waited to pick up any jumper.

Smart.

As her feet touched the water a gust of wind caught the parachute full blast, dragging her like a rag doll along the river straight toward an outcropping of boulders.

Holt raced along the edge and then splashed into the shallow depths on a diagonal path to the woman struggling to release the harness.

Ten feet to go. The water was now waist high. Five feet. He lunged.

Cold water sprayed, blinding him, but he had a handful of fabric. He dug his heels into the soft riverbed and braced himself. The force of the wind-dragged parachute jerked his shoulder, but he held on.

He blinked until he could see. He had her by one of the chest straps. She reached up and gripped his wrist.

Step by precarious step, he eased backward. When he reached the shallows, the woman scrabbled for and found her footing. Circling his other arm around her waist, he hauled her up against his body and held on.

Beside him Ted jumped into the water and made his way over to the chute lines. Others joined him and worked to collapse the parachute.

Holt reached between their bodies and released the clasp and slipped the straps over her shoulders. She shimmied out of the harness, but as she stepped clear, she tripped, stumbling against him. He staggered and lost his footing. Together they fell.

He hit the ground, the jolt sending a hiss of pain through his clenched teeth. The jumper sprawled on top of him.

"Hey, are you all right?" Concern filled her voice. Elbows and knees, one dangerously close to causing him real pain, flayed as she struggled to move off him.

"Hold still." He managed to sit up and found himself face-to-face with her straddling his lap. Incredibly, laughter filled the bright blue eyes as she scrutinized him. Her soft body shifted, causing an altogether different physical reaction, as she reached up and removed her helmet.

Honey-blond hair tumbled across her shoulders as she gave him a bright smile. "That was sooo awesome! I can't believe that I just jumped a three-hundred-and-forty-five-million-year-old gorge."

He didn't know whether to dump her back in the river or kiss her.

"Oh, by the way." She extended a slender hand and, bemused, he gripped it. A strange sensation surged along his arm as if a circuit had been completed and her life force was pumping into him at a million bits a second.

"I'm Emma-Lee Dalton."

EMMA-LEE HAD DONE IT. She had jumped for her friend Sandy.

When her friend was physically strong enough again after the chemotherapy, they would go parachuting together. Those moments of absolute freedom from all earthly ties might be the ticket to boost Sandy's spirits.

With the adrenaline rush still fizzing in her veins like champagne, Emma-Lee grinned at the man whose lap she straddled. Of course, this man who had charged into the river and dragged her to safety could definitely get a woman's blood pounding. When he failed to reciprocate with his name, she arched a brow.

"I believe our—" she gave a meaningful glance down "—circumstances warrant an introduction?"

The way he studied her with such intense hazel eyes sent a delicious shiver through her having nothing to do with the fact that she was drenched. His was a strong, lean face, softened only by a frame of damp waves of hair. A sculpted mouth that could lend itself only too easily to brooding. She couldn't help but notice that his stomach was board flat and he had hard, muscled thighs.

As he continued to regard her in silence, she realized here was a man who valued self-possession. An age-old awareness stirred within her, raising a very feminine challenge. What would it be like to be the woman who caused him to lose control?

Heat pooling deep inside her chased away the bone-deep chill from the river lapping around them. Even though logically Emma-Lee knew he couldn't know the direction of her thoughts, embarrassment overrode her mind and warmth infused her cheeks. His eyes narrowed and then for the first time he smiled like a predator that had run his prey to ground. She was in trouble.

"I'm Holt Forrester."

This was Holt Forrester? Not at all like the geeky teenage computer genius made good she had envisioned from his Internet bio.

His voice was dark and quiet, as she remembered from their phone conversation.

"I don't know about you, but I'm freezing my butt off in this water. Could we continue this conversation under better conditions?" he said.

"Oh, sorry." Mortified, she scrambled to her feet. He followed suit and then, gripping her elbow, guided her up the bank. A young man carrying blankets rushed up.

"Thanks, Ted." Holt took one and wrapped it around her shoulders.

"Over in the lot we have a motor home that we're using as a control center. Let's get you inside and get you warmed up. Do you have a change of clothes? If not, I can send Ted to get you some."

"You don't need to go to any trouble. I have a bag in my car, but I'm parked at the Cliffhanger Lodge. If you could point me in the direction of the shuttle—"

"Don't be ridiculous. You'll catch pneumonia. Give me your keys and a description of the car, and I'll see if Ted can bring back your car while you take a hot shower."

A stranger drive her precious car on that poor excuse of a road running from the river to the highway? No way.

"Thank you, but the shocks would never survive the trip down." She smiled at the younger man. "However, if you wouldn't mind, I'd be eternally grateful if you could retrieve my bag."

Ted nodded. "I'd be happy to get it for you."

This time the shiver that racked her system had nothing to do with hormones. She was cold.

Emma-Lee unzipped the pocket of her jumpsuit and after removing her keys, handed them over. Holt tossed them to Ted and she gave the assistant a description of her car along with the tag number. Ted hurried off.

"This way." Holt guided her and propelled her to the parking area where an enormous black motor home occupied one end. Had she really expected a mobile home along the lines of the cheerful red one that her parents owned? This monster was closer to the one her sister Mallory and her race car driver husband, Roberto Castillo, used at the races.

Holt led her up the steps, opened the door and urged her inside. She blinked until her vision adjusted. The living-dining room area buzzed with activity. Some people sat on tan leather benches at laptops stationed around a long table, while others stood talking on phones or radios. Several TVs were mounted on walls with flashing pictures of the bridge and exhibition stands. Now she knew why the event had gone with military-like precision. Holt had left nothing to chance.

Although a few individuals, particularly women, looked at her with curiosity, most kept focused on the task at hand. A well-trained crew, she thought.

Holt weaved a path toward the rear and slid open a door. Incredibly, a king-size bed with a black-and-tan silk spread dominated the bedroom. A black entertainment unit along the opposite wall contained yet another large TV, along with stereo equipment and high-tech video game remotes. A modernistic chrome-and-glass chandelier glittered to life when he flipped the switch. The interior designer had certainly decorated to masculine tastes, Emma-Lee wryly thought as she spied a well-stocked minibar with a champagne bucket on top. A man bent on seduction wouldn't have to leave the room.

"Nice motor home, Holt."

He shook his head. "It's not mine. A loaner from a friend." He walked along the narrow pass-through to the left of the bed.

"Even comes with two complete bathrooms, so why don't you use this one." He opened a door. "There are plenty of towels and a robe you can use until Ted returns with your bag."

"Thank you."

When he continued to hold the door, she scooted past him, her body brushing against his. Despite her better sense, she looked up. His face was close, so close that if she stood on her toes she could kiss him…

His nostrils flared as if he could read her thoughts, and he braced his hands on either side of her, effectively trapping her against the door.

"Are you going to need help getting out of the jumpsuit? The zipper's been soaked."

Laughing, she put her hands against his chest and shoved. "I can manage just fine."

He let his hands drop and stepped back. "Call if you change your mind."

With a sweet smile she closed the door in his face without replying. Then she sagged against it.

Ohmigod. What a close call. With one searing glance he could turn a woman's brains to mush.

Shaking her head, she straightened, let the soggy

blanket drop to the floor, and grabbed the zipper tab on her jumpsuit.

And tugged. Nothing. She jerked again. The darn thing wouldn't budge. Sighing, she turned and tapped her forehead against the door.

"Emma-Lee?" Holt's voice sounded dangerously close on the other side. "Are you all right?"

No way would she open the door, let alone concede he had been right. "I'm fine!" she called out. "I rapped my elbow, that's all."

She flipped the lock on the door and gazed around the bathroom. There. Liquid soap. She pumped a glob onto her fingers and worked the slimy stuff over the zipper. She almost cried with relief when the tab pulled down without further resistance.

Five minutes later, after a steamy shower, Emma-Lee felt like a new woman. She slipped into a plush, white cotton robe and opened the door. Her breath froze in her lungs.

On the opposite side dressed only in worn jeans, Holt stood pulling on a black V-neck sweater. Tanned skin stretched tightly over his rib cage. Oh, yeah. She had been right about his having a toned physique.

His head popped through the opening, and he spotted her at once. As he drew the sweater down, he gave her a slow smile.

"I see you managed without me, what a shame."

"Yes." She drew the robe close around her throat in a protective gesture.

He ran his fingers through his damp hair. "Your bag's on the bed. I'll leave you to change." With a last look, he left the room.

Emma-Lee hummed as she opened the bag and took out her change of clothes. Something sharp pricked her finger, and she froze as she starred at the pink-ribbon pin attached to the shirt.

Guilt sliced through Emma-Lee's elation. Here she was again, having a great time and flirting with a good-looking man while her friend was probably still puking from her chemo session yesterday.

So much for her grandiose decision to get serious with her life after Sandy had given her the tearful news that the cancer she had battled during their college days had returned.

Cancer was so unfair. Sandy had so much to live for, a husband, baby and career, while Emma-Lee hadn't accomplished anything with her life…

Stop it. Emma-Lee drew in a long, deep breath. There's nothing you can do about cancer's capriciousness. All you do is offer support. Sandy would beat this recurrence; she had to.

She would grab a quick meal with her BASE jumping friends and the NASCAR fans she had met here as she promised before heading up to her room. Then she would call Sandy and give her a full-blown account of the day.

Emma-Lee repacked the bag with her wet clothes and slung it over her shoulder. She slid open the door and spotted Holt at the front, speaking with Ted. All the other people were gone. He had put on a battered leather jacket, and his hair was mussed as if he had been outside. She made her way to them.

"Ted, you're a lifesaver. Thank you for getting my bag."

"You're welcome, ma'am. Here are your keys." He grinned and then left.

Left alone, Holt faced her. His gaze leisurely skimmed her from top to bottom, and her face warmed under the potent survey.

"I…wanted to…" She halted, swallowed and started again. "Thank you for everything. I'll get out of your way."

He lifted a shoulder. "No hurry. As you can see, we're actually wrapping up. The auction's about over. I should be the one thanking you for all the donations you brought from Double S Racing. Can I buy you dinner?"

More time with him. The idea was alluring, but she had given her word and then there was Sandy. Emma-Lee shook her head.

"Sorry, but I promised my friends I would meet them at the hotel's restaurant before I head home."

He stiffened as if he was drawing back into himself, but he said nothing further. Instead, he reached around her to open the door. She went through it, hunching her shoulders against the wind. He followed her down the steps.

He walked over to the black truck next to the motor home and opened the door. After she slid inside, he shut the door and got in the driver's side and started the engine. The drive up what passed for a winding road to the bridge was spent in silence. Since Holt appeared to be deep in thought, Emma-Lee occupied herself with watching the amazing vista. At the top of the gorge Holt took the side road leading to the Cliffhanger Lodge and stopped before the entrance.

She opened her mouth to say goodbye but instead blurted, "You're welcome to join us for dinner. Combine a bunch of BASE jumpers with NASCAR fans, it should be a wild time."

Although his expression lightened, he shook his head. "Sorry, but I'm not much into big groups."

The sharp cut of disappointment surprised her. "Oh, okay. It was a pleasure meeting you." She held out her hand.

With a quick move that surprised her, Holt lifted her hand to his mouth and pressed a kiss to the palm. Her skin tingled as little pulses of excitement danced over it. As his lips lingered, an intense awareness that was almost painful jolted her. Of their own volition her fingers curled.

Before she could collect her thoughts, he released her hand. She pulled it back to safety and wrapped her arm around her middle. He sat staring at her with narrowed eyes as if he was trying to analyze a puzzle.

Aware she was way over her head, Emma-Lee drew in a shuddering breath and struggled for a nonchalant tone. Little had she realized when she had wondered what it would be like to shake his self-possession that she would be playing with fire. If she wasn't careful, she could get singed.

"What was that about?"

A slow, dangerous smile curved his mouth. "At the river I didn't know whether to toss you back into the water or kiss you."

Huh. Right now she was edgy enough to dunk him all over again, but she unbuckled her safety belt, opened the door and got out.

"Emma-Lee."

She looked over her shoulder at Holt. He sat silhouetted against the deepening twilight, but she saw the flash of his grin.

"I'm glad I caught you."

CHAPTER TWO

CONSTRUCTED OF TIMBER and glass, and perched on a cliff, the Cliffhanger Lodge had a sweeping deck with a killer view of the New River Gorge. Every room had been taken for the weekend by either the event's staff or participants. Now that the jump was over, partying was the order of the night.

Holt stood outside the lodge's glass-walled restaurant, watching the well-lit scene before him. At a wood table in the corner, Emma-Lee sat smiling amid a large group of people, mainly male admirers.

How he ended up here, he wasn't sure. After all, with the jumping over, all that remained was the partying. He'd completed the last pass to make sure all the exhibition booths had closed and checked in with the local authorities. And what he'd told Emma-Lee was true. He didn't gravitate to big groups. But rather than getting in his car and heading to the airport, he found himself here.

He still had time to make it back to Atlanta and catch a late-night dinner with Marguerite, his latest female acquaintance. She wouldn't care the hour he showed up. An aspiring model, she liked his connections and they suited each other in the physical department. More important, she fit in well with his lifestyle: companionship with no emotional ties.

Pulling out his state-of-the-art smartphone, he checked his messages. One was from Marguerite asking if she should expect him. The restaurant's door swung open, and warmth and laughter came rushing toward him as a couple walked out arm in arm. At the large table, a man sitting next to Emma-Lee draped an arm around the back of her chair. Whatever he said caused her to laugh. The man rose and headed toward the bar.

Holt texted a one-word response—no—put away the device and walked inside. Several people recognizing him gave a shout-out. Emma-Lee looked over and he held her gaze as he approached the table. He finessed the chair next to her as its former occupant approached with two beers in hand.

"Hey, buddy, that's my—" The man, one of the town's chamber of commerce members that Holt had dealt with, halted. "Holt."

"Hi, Burt." Holt indicated the table. "If you could flag down a waiter, I'd be happy to buy a round for everyone here."

Although Burt wore an irritated expression, the rest of the group broke out in cheers.

As Emma-Lee took her foaming mug from Burt, she said, "Let me introduce you."

Without a glitch, not only did she announce everyone's name, but also gave him an identification tag as to why they were here. A Florida couple had made the trip because the husband's mother had cancer. Another from a neighboring West Virginia town had come for a chance at NASCAR memorabilia. The man proudly displayed a pair of tickets for the Richmond race while his wife tipped her Linc Shepherd cap.

"Emma-Lee said she would get us his autograph."

"You bet," Emma-Lee assured them.

"This is his year to take the NASCAR Sprint Cup Series," added the husband.

"No way. Bart Branch's going to take it." A man sitting across from him leaned forward.

"In your dreams. It's Jeb Stallworth's all the way," announced another man. A vigorous debate erupted around the table.

Feeling like a fish out of water, Holt leaned back and contented himself by watching Emma-Lee's animated expressions as she followed the discussion.

She threw a puzzled glance in his direction. "What?"

He lifted a shoulder. "You look right at home here."

She sipped her beer. "It reminds me of a very upscale Maudie's with all the warmth and home cooking."

"Who's Maudie?"

Laughing, Emma-Lee set down the mug. "Not who. What. Maudie's Down Home Diner in Mooresville, North Carolina, where I live. It's the racing crowd's secret place where everyone hangs out. I end up eating there most nights."

"Why NASCAR?"

A burst of raucous laughter came from the next table. Emma-Lee frowned. "Sorry, I didn't hear what you said."

Holt leaned closer to her. "Want to go outside for air?"

She regarded him for a minute before nodding. He snagged a passing waitress, handed her money for the table's tab plus a generous tip and then rose. Emma-Lee followed suit, wishing everyone a safe trip if she didn't see them again.

Outside they headed in mutual accord toward the side facing the bridge. The cold front had swept in, bringing a decided nip to the spring night. A quarter moon hung high in the sky blazing with stars.

"Lovely night," Emma-Lee commented.

Great. He sucked royally at small talk. "Inside I asked why you're working for NASCAR. For a race car owner."

Her lips quirked. "More than an owner of a race car. Gil Sizemore has four teams."

"You know what I mean."

"Yes, I do." She kicked a small pebble, sending it skittering across the pavement.

"I grew up around racing. My parents are total gearheads. They still drive their mobile home to every race they can. Then my sisters Tara and Mallory married into NASCAR."

The surname clicked. "Dalton. Of course. Your sisters are the author Tara Dalton and the actress Mallory Dalton."

"Yes." She lifted a shoulder. "Through them I met Gil at a race. I was at loose ends, needed a change, and he offered me a job as his personal assistant. Little did I know that I was getting myself on the hook for being on call twenty-four hours a day."

Although Holt never mixed business with pleasure, he knew other men who did. An unexpected shaft of jealousy speared through him. "Is he your boyfriend?"

Emma-Lee halted and fisted her hands on her hips. "Excuse me?"

"I thought because you're together—"

She stabbed her finger into his chest. "I play guard dog to his office, answer phones, deal with correspondence, run errands, and when I attend races, help out wherever needed, but the job description does not…"

She poked again for emphasis. "Does not include being his girlfriend. Clear?"

Holt grabbed her hand before she could inflict any more damage. "Clear."

Although she tugged to get free, he held on to her hand and leaned against the railing. Her eyes were dark as she regarded him.

"What about you? Any attachments?"

"Nothing ever permanent." Before she could press him further, he said, "Tell me more about NASCAR."

He might as well get more information from someone actually working in that world, not to mention beautiful and definitely entertaining. After all, Stan Preston was on the outside looking in and might not have the most accurate perspective.

"You don't follow it?"

"Not until recently. I haven't even attended a race yet."

"Richmond's coming up next weekend. Would you like to go? I might be able to get you a pass to the garage and pit road."

As simple as that, his opportunity to study close at hand the inner dynamics of a race team fell into his lap. He could make up his mind about sponsoring Preston's venture and see Emma-Lee again under casual circumstances. No ties, no expectations. Just the way he preferred.

"I'd like that, but only if you're going to be there."

She flashed a smile. "You're in luck. Although the higher administrative types run the show at the race, my boss needs me there to help out."

"Then we have a deal."

When she shook his hand he was still holding hers, with reluctance he released her. She moved to stand by him at the railing and together they stood looking at the vista. Here and there lights dusted the valley, but below the abyss was dark and still as death.

Darkness could hide a multitude of emotions and fears. Ever since his mother's death, he'd been hell-bent at pushing at life's limits, by racing, jumping or skiing. However, there was a fine line between the temporary oblivion an adrenaline rush brought and a death wish. Some days he didn't know if he cared about the difference.

"Why did you jump today?" he asked in a quiet tone. This was the answer he really sought from her.

She stared down at the void. "Why does anyone jump? For the thrill of it."

"I don't buy that. I know that you met the number of jumps as a parachutist in order to qualify to BASE jump, so obviously you're an experienced jumper. But you could have stayed in your safe little office at Mooresville and sent me everything. Instead, you threw yourself into this fundraiser today. Why?"

The night cast deep shadows across her face when she turned. "I know someone battling cancer. My best friend from college."

"You could have made a donation. Helped with the stands. Why take the risk?"

"Because of the guilt that I'm alive and healthy," she whispered.

He'd been racing from that guilt trip ever since his mother died. Emma-Lee's confirmation of what he felt every time he jumped ripped free his own response. "Exactly."

Suddenly needing to explore further the taste of her skin he'd gotten from kissing her palm earlier, he lowered his head.

From the other side of the veranda, spotlights blazed, music blared and the Black Eyed Peas were singing "Boom Boom Pow." Emma-Lee started. "What's that?"

Holt gave her a rueful smile. "That would be the portable vertical wind tunnel."

"Oh, wow!" She clapped her hands with excitement. "A wind tunnel that allows you to float in the air? Can we try it?"

As people spilled onto the veranda, any hope he had of a kiss and maybe more evaporated. He wrapped his arm around her shoulders. "Since I'm the one who rented it, you can be the first."

Note to self for next year's event: arrange for the wind tunnel to run only during the day. A mere mortal man apparently couldn't compete for a kiss in the shadows of the night against the thrill of flying, not when it came to a woman like Emma-Lee.

EARLY SUNDAY MORNING Holt leaned against a column hewn from timber in the glass-enclosed lobby of the Cliffhanger Lodge. Even he would have to admit for once in his life he was dawdling. There were a lot of things he could be doing, from checking messages to reading reports; instead, he was simply waiting.

Banners and signs about the charity event still decorated the lobby. Around him trickles of guests headed either into the restaurant for breakfast or stood in line to check out. Conversation still buzzed about the BASE jump and the partying afterward.

"Man, did you see that trio who did the synchronized flips?… The wind tunnel rocked last night… I won a Rafael O'Bryan T-shirt."

Smiling, Holt shifted as he glanced at his watch. His assistant, Ted, was still in the restaurant, running the thank-you breakfast for the volunteers. One benefit of having his own jet, it would take off whenever he was ready to leave.

And go where? Back to another empty hotel room?

Well, wasn't that a self-pitying thought?

Irritated with himself, he straightened and moved away from the column. He was living the life he wanted, with no ties, able to pick up and go wherever his next venture took him. The restless mood plaguing him since he had left Emma-Lee last night was only a symptom of the letdown from the adrenaline rush after pulling off the fundraiser in his mother's memory. Come tomorrow, he'd be wrapped up in meetings for his new computer venture.

His phone rang, momentarily giving him a welcome respite from his strange mood, until he saw the caller identification.

"Hello, Dad." He moved away from a group of laughing women. Concern pricked him as he could count on one hand the number of times either he or Sam Forrester would actually call the other during the year—Thanksgiving, Christmas and each other's birthdays.

"What's wrong?"

"Why does anything have to be wrong, son?" Sam's voice held a familiar note of perplexed exasperation. His father had often sounded that way in dealing with a son he didn't understand and a reality he hadn't wanted.

"I'm calling because I saw you on the news last night."

Holt blinked. Since when had his father ever emerged from his academia cocoon long enough to watch television? Did he even own a set?

Sam Forrester continued, "The reporter indicated the event drew in a large crowd."

"Yes, it went very well." He walked to a point in the lobby where he could keep an eye on both the outside and the bank of elevators.

"You named it in your mother's honor."

If Sam had read one of the e-mails he had sent when he had first conceived of the event… Holt rolled his shoulders to ease the building tension. "That's right."

"Amanda would have been proud of you, Holt."

And what about you, Dad? He wanted to ask but knew it was pointless. After all, no matter how many times he had brought home straight A's on his report card or scholastic awards, Sam had always reacted as if such accomplishments were expected. The word praise wasn't in his vocabulary.

"Thanks, Dad." Out of the corner of his eye he spotted an elevator opening. Emma-Lee, carrying her bag, exited with several others. A man said something to her and she laughed, the warm, silky sound rippling along his nerve endings.

She was leaving. Suddenly, Holt realized that he had to spend more time with her. Today. He didn't want to wait until next weekend. He needed to come up with a plan and quick.

He knew her car was here, so he couldn't offer Emma-Lee a lift home. However...

As an idea formed, his mouth kicked up at the corner. The jet would go wherever he needed it to.

"Dad, I'm sorry, but I have to go. Something's come up."

"But—" There was a second of silence. "Sure, son. I know you're a busy man."

Rather than hitting the disconnect button, Holt hesitated. His father sounded weary. "Dad, you okay?"

"I'm fine. I'll speak with you later."

"Sure thing. I'll e-mail you when I get back to Atlanta."

"Bye, Holt."

The moment his father had hung up, Holt was texting his assistant. He prayed Ted wouldn't pick this inopportune moment to emerge from the restaurant. Instructions delivered, Holt clipped the phone to his belt and moved on a diagonal to intercept Emma-Lee. As he rounded the last group of people separating them, she saw him and a smile lit up her face.

There. Holt experienced the same kick of anticipation he had whenever he jumped from a plane or raced a bike or had a breakthrough on a computer program. This was what he had been waiting for all morning.

Never before had a woman been the source of such an acute rush.

That realization alone should have given him pause, but Holt never backed down from a challenge. He closed the last few feet as Emma-Lee pulled a ringing cell phone from her purse.

CHAPTER THREE

HOLT WAS HERE.

An awareness so intense that it bordered on pain jolted Emma-Lee's nerve endings. He moved toward her with easy masculine grace. Today his hazel eyes took on the cast of the dark gold shirt he wore along with jeans hugging his lean form and a bomber jacket.

Those serious eyes held her own almost against her will as he drew closer.

Phone. It was ringing in the tone that signaled her mother was calling. She wrenched her gaze away, set down her bag and answered the cell.

"Hi, Mom. Happy Sunday."

"Hi, honey. Are you all right? I know you were doing that insane jump yesterday. When you didn't call, your father was practically frantic with worry."

Oops. While she had called her friend Sandy last night to regale her with details of the day and the fascinating man she had met, she had forgotten to call her parents. Guilt pricked her. That was so unlike her not to call. She knew her parents were concerned about her riskier leisure activities.

In the background on Shirley Dalton's end of the line, her father's muffled voice protested. "Oh, hush, Buddy," her mother ordered. "You, too, were worried about her."

"Mom, I'm fine. I just forgot to call you. I'm sorry."

"Nothing broken? No cuts or bruises?"

Emma-Lee laughed. "I'm fine. Not even a scratch." She

wouldn't mention the near miss with the river boulders. "I'm one hundred percent intact."

Glancing at Holt, she stilled. His gaze lazily drifted down the length of her and back up again. A shiver raced through her when he gave her a wicked smile along with a thumbs-up. She glared at him before turning away so she could concentrate.

"Look, Mom. I'm checking out. I'll call you and Dad tonight and give you all the details."

"All right, dear. Drive safe. Stop a few times to stretch your legs. You're too much like your father. Once you get in a car, all you want to do is drive until you reach your destination. It's not good for you."

Emma-Lee rolled her eyes. "Yes, Mom. Bye." She hung up and turned back to Holt.

As she pocketed the phone, she gave him an apologetic smile. "My folks were worried. You know how parents like to fuss."

He gave her a strange, questioning look. "If you say so."

Over his shoulder she saw a banner hanging over the entrance: The Amanda Forrester Jump for Cancer. Horror rushed through her as she realized the connection.

All she had seen when Holt's donation query came in to Double S was that his event was for cancer. Not the actual name. With visions of bridge jumping when she had checked in and images of the intriguing man himself dancing in her head afterward, she had been oblivious to any sign.

"Ohmigod." She lifted her hands and covered her face. "Amanda Forrester, the woman this event is for. Is she your mother?"

"Was." A cool, shuttered expression appeared in his eyes. "She's dead."

"Oh, Holt. I'm so sorry." She reached and rested her hand on his forearm. Beneath her fingers the tendons were as taut as steel. She could feel the tension humming through him.

He slid his hands into his jean pockets, so she was forced to let go. "That's okay. She died from cancer a long time ago."

"How old were you when you lost her?"

"Twelve."

She couldn't imagine losing a parent at that age—or any age for that matter. Her parents were her rock and foundation.

"How awful for you and your father!" Emma-Lee hesitated. "Your father is…"

"Still alive, yes." He nodded. "We muddled through mother's death, but I had always wanted to do something in her memory."

She gave him a tremulous smile. "And you pulled it off. This was a truly memorable weekend, Holt, for all of us who got to participate. An honor, in fact. Thank you."

Surprise flickered across his face. "I should thank you for all the help you gave me." He glanced at her suitcase. "Are you checking out?"

She nodded. "Yes. I need to get going. I want to visit with a friend in Charlotte before I head home."

"Really, Charlotte?" Holt narrowed his eyes. "Can I be this lucky? Ted left with the car to take care of an urgent matter this morning, and I need to get to Charlotte to meet with a programmer. I was waiting down here while they located another rental car for me. I wonder if I could…"

Her sympathy propelled by manners caused her to respond without thinking. "Of course, I'm happy to give you a lift."

"Perfect." He reached out and grabbed the handle of her suitcase. "Let's get you checked out." He turned toward the reception desk but not before she caught a glint of satisfaction in his eyes.

Any lingering trace of compassion vanished. What had she gotten herself into? Several hours of driving with a man she still didn't know well?

Oh, boy. Another thing not to mention to her parents tonight. However...

Emma-Lee pulled out her phone, snapped a picture of Holt as he approached a clerk and e-mailed it to Sandy along with a note of what time she would be arriving as a precaution.

When Holt glanced back, she dropped the phone into her purse and hurried forward. She noted the clerk's name tag as she slid her key card across the counter. "Good morning, Trevor. I'm all set." Within short order she completed the check-out process.

Holt gestured toward the door. "I need to pick up my bag from the bell captain and we can be on our way."

She nodded and threaded her way through the growing crowd checking out. After only a few moments' delay Holt had his duffel bag and they went outside. She inhaled a deep breath of the crisp spring air. Only a few wisps of clouds drifted across the blue sky. What a glorious day for driving. She led the way to the parking lot.

"You didn't valet?" Holt asked as he walked beside her.

"Not when I can avoid it. A good car deserves respect that many kids don't have." She halted by the vintage, fire-engine-red Mustang and ran a loving hand over the fender. "This is Baby. The first car I bought with my own money."

Holt cocked an eyebrow. "You named your car?"

"Of course." She popped the trunk and he placed their bags inside. After she closed the lid, she turned. Holt stood with his hand out.

"What?"

"Can I drive?"

In mock horror she clutched them close to her chest. "Oh, no. I don't know you well enough to allow that familiarity."

He grinned and leaned against the car. He didn't budge when she glared at him. "So who's allowed to drive Baby?"

She strode past him and opened the driver's door. "My

parents, my sisters and my best friend." She wanted to feel the wind in her hair, so she rolled the window down. When it was time to retire Baby…not that that would be for a long time, she patted the dashboard in reassurance…her next car would be a convertible.

Holt caught the door handle and shut it for her. He rounded the front and got in the passenger side. After buckling his belt, he studied her. "What about boyfriends? Any of them ever drive her?"

"Nope."

"Good." Holt adjusted the seat, settled back and actually closed his eyes.

Men. She placed her phone beside her, started the engine, smiled with pleasure at the smooth purr of the engine, and eased out of the space. She carefully drove along the narrow graveled road from the hotel and only relaxed when she pulled onto the paved highway.

Quickly the miles peeled away as they rode in silence. Occasionally, she stole a look at Holt. Although he appeared to be dozing, she was acutely aware of his presence in the cramped space. Despite the open windows, the warm musk of his scent toyed with her nose.

"So who's this friend you're going to see in Charlotte?" When she glanced over, his head was turned and he was watching her intently.

She cleared her throat. "My best friend, Sandy. She's the one I jumped for yesterday."

"She has cancer?"

"Yes. The first time she was diagnosed was when we were in college. She kept up with her classes despite the chemo-therapy. We thought she had beaten it, but she recently had a relapse."

"I'm sorry to hear that."

Sorry didn't begin to cover Emma-Lee's reaction when

Sandy had told her the heartbreaking news. She balled her right hand in her lap. "She'll beat it again, she's strong."

Holt reached out and squeezed her hand. "They've come a long way with the research, Emma-Lee."

She bit her lip and nodded. "I know."

The phone beside her erupted in a song heavy with bass and drum. She smiled. "Speak of the devil." She reached for it, but Holt grabbed the phone first.

"Hey!"

"You're driving," he chided, opening the phone. Her face turned warm as he stared at his photo on the screen. Slowly his mouth curved with satisfaction.

"Don't let your ego get the wrong idea," she snapped. "I sent Sandy your photo in case something happened to me."

EMMA-LEE'S BALD statement landed a solid punch to Holt's solar plexus. He sucked in a deep breath as he battled the strange sting of hurt and struggled to assimilate the thought that she could be afraid of him. Her phone fell silent.

When he thought he could speak calmly, he said in a quiet voice, "Emma-Lee, I thought we had hit it off and were getting to know each other. Why did you let me ride with you if you're worried about me?"

A deep pink flush crept over her face and when she glanced at him, remorse welled in the deep blue pools of her eyes. "Oh, Holt. I'm sorry. I didn't mean it that way."

The phone erupted again in the same throbbing song. "Why don't you pull over. I have a feeling your friend is going to keep calling until you answer."

She nodded, signaled and carefully drove onto the side of the highway. Holt answered the phone, "Sandy? This is Holt Forrester."

"Where's Emma-Lee? Is she all right?" Concern was sharp

in the woman's voice. "If anything's happened to her, so help me, I will track you down and—"

"Hold on. Do you have videoconferencing?"

"Yes."

"Then turn it on." He pressed a button and turned the screen toward Emma-Lee, who gave a weak smile.

"Hi, Sandy, I'm fine. Truly. I was driving and needed to pull over."

"I want to see Holt."

"Demanding, isn't she?" he murmured before turning the phone back to him. Although the resolution wasn't state-of-the-art, Sandy's visage showed a pretty woman with fine-boned features, although a tad too thin. She wore a bright scarf tied around her head.

Holt's stomach twisted. His mother had born the same too-gaunt look during her chemotherapy sessions. Back then, though, the fashion had been wigs rather than the more defiant scarves women wore today. Amanda Forrester had made a game of it, wearing different-colored wigs to emulate women actors.

He shook off the memory and smiled. "Sandy, nice to meet you."

The woman stared at him so intensely he wondered if she was trying to see to his soul. Good luck with that.

Then, as if she had come to a decision, she gave a brisk nod. "You're the Mr. Amazing who came to Emma-Lee's rescue yesterday?"

The tension he'd been experiencing since Emma-Lee's comment about the photo began to ease. He'd never been anybody's "amazing." "I helped. I'm not sure Emma-Lee ever needs rescuing."

Sandy snorted. "You got that right. She's too busy help-ing others to ask for it herself. However, thank you. I don't think even she could have come out unscathed from a close encounter with boulders."

"You're welcome."

"Give me that." Emma-Lee snatched the phone, opened the door and got out. He watched her pace back and forth as she spoke with her friend. Apparently, the only time she was at rest was when she was driving.

Several minutes later his door opened. Biting her lip, Emma-Lee tapped the phone against the palm of her hand. "Would you mind driving for a while? I'm suddenly tired."

She was allowing him to drive her precious car. Her peace offering of trust shook him to his core. He unbuckled his belt and got out of the car. When he stood, he was within a kiss's breath of her. The spring breeze swept honey tendrils of hair across her face that she pushed back impatiently.

He curved his hands around her shoulders and watched with delight as nerves darted into her eyes, darkening them. Her lips parted, and he desired nothing more than to taste them. However, he didn't want to ruin her gesture of faith, so instead he pressed a kiss to her forehead.

"Thank you. I promise that I will take good care of Baby."

She swallowed and stepped away from him. "You'd better."

He held the door and she slid inside. A minute later he turned the engine, appreciating its well-tuned power. The rest of the trip to Charlotte was spent with surprisingly easy small talk. At the exit for the airport, Holt turned.

Emma-Lee sat up. "Aren't we going to Sandy's house?"

Seeing cancer-ravaged Sandy's image had stirred enough ghosts that haunted him. He didn't think he could handle meeting her in person.

He said easily, "The programmer I told you about is flying in, so I'll meet with him here. That way I can catch the first flight to Atlanta once we're done. I'll pull up to the curb and you can be on your way to Sandy's."

"I see." She linked her fingers in her lap and stared out the window.

He pulled up in front of the terminal, got out and retrieved his bag from the trunk. As Emma-Lee passed him to go to the driver's side, he caught her elbow.

"Emma-Lee. I look forward to seeing you at Richmond."

She nodded, took a step away, and then swung back. She stood on her tiptoes and kissed his cheek. Before he could react, she darted to the driver's side and got inside, shutting the door. Then the car roared off, leaving him standing bemused.

He touched the side of his face still tingling from the touch of her lips before he picked up his bag and slung it over his shoulder. Something was happening to him, but now was not the time to analyze it. Without Emma-Lee's vibrant presence, the emotional fatigue he had been holding off since the conclusion of the jump was setting in.

He pulled out his phone and checked his messages. The jet was already here, waiting for him. Good. Although it was a short hike to the landing field for private aircraft, he decided he needed to stretch his legs after the long drive. As he walked, he scanned the other messages, frowning when he saw one from his father only thirty minutes old. Maybe the fundraiser for Amanda had opened the coffin lid on his father's memories, as well.

Holt hesitated and then pocketed the phone. He would open the message later. Although the jump had awakened old memories, he had anticipated them. However, seeing Emma-Lee's friend had rubbed him rawer than he'd expected.

Cancer's scars ran deep, not only for those afflicted, but also for those left behind.

CHAPTER FOUR

SATURDAY AFTERNOON and excitement pumped through the Richmond garage area as people dashed and darted all over the place. The air snapped, crackled and popped with intensity. Two hours before the Richmond race and in the final countdown the teams were readying their cars.

Commandeered by Marley Sizemore, Gil's sister and sponsor relations for Double S Racing, Emma-Lee chatted with a group of sponsors and their friends while keeping a puzzled eye on Holt standing next to a computer station.

Although she had introduced him to everyone in the group Marley had assigned her, he hadn't mixed in. Clearly, meeting one of Double S's drivers, getting an autograph or waxing poetic over the car's paint job wasn't the ticket to keeping his interest. The moment he'd spotted a crew member working a computer, he'd split apart.

Last time she had sidled close enough to listen, he had been asking questions about aerodynamics, weather and track conditions. Once a computer geek, always a computer geek. However, with his wavy dark blond hair, chiseled features, rangy build, he could have been mistaken for a driver.

Still, she had pegged him right last Saturday. If you scratched past the charming smile and professional manners, Holt Forrester was a loner. His statement that he never had any permanent attachments in relationships should be a yellow flag. Maybe for once in her life she should observe the caution her family was always pleading for her to use.

Then again, maybe she should bone up on computers. After all, he had called and e-mailed her nearly every day.

"Ms. Dalton." The pained, dazed expression on a middle-aged man standing beside her clued her in at once.

"Oh, I'm sorry. Was I spotting off too many facts?"

Others nodded while he flushed. "I'm afraid the degrees of the track's banking are over my head. However, could you tell me the track's inaugural year? I have a dinner bet riding with my son."

"Certainly, 1953."

"I thought so." The man pulled out a cell phone and occupied himself with texting.

"Since the garage is the heartbeat of Double S's racing operations, I'll let you observe and absorb the preparations. If you have any questions, please don't hesitate to ask me."

Keeping a watchful eye on her charges, Emma-Lee stood to the group's side. To date, her favorite assignment at Double S Racing was filling in for the charity coordinator while she was out on maternity leave. There had been nothing like the sense of satisfaction when Holt had called and told her how much money the racing donations had raised.

However, if Marley was going to entrust her with helping out with sponsors on race day, she was going to have to be careful with her information dumps.

As a teenager, exasperated by the "you're blonde so therefore you must be dumb" assumption, she'd thrown herself into learning. Facts had become her defense against stereotyping. How often growing up had she heard Tara labeled as the brains, Mallory the beauty and herself the personality as others discussed the Dalton sisters?

However, Emma-Lee's secret was she loved knowledge although not necessarily the type gleaned only from books. Sometimes you had to experience life in order to fully comprehend black-and-white facts.

A woman dripping in gold and diamonds broke away from the pack and approached her. Although Emma-Lee kept a polite smile plastered on her face, she tensed. A sponsor's wife, Tammy Ray always acted as if she owned the teams herself.

The woman simpered. "I wanted a chance to chat with you, Emma-Lee, since I know both of your sisters so well."

Not likely, since Tara and Mallory avoided Tammy Ray like the plague at any NASCAR event.

Tammy fanned herself with a glossy brochure Marley Sizemore had handed out earlier. "You must be so proud of your sister Mallory. It's hard to believe she was once America's Sweetheart."

Then the woman gave a faint shudder. "Now she's up for all those acting awards for such a dark movie."

"Mallory's a wonderful actor and she knocked that role out of the park." Pride resonated in Emma-Lee's voice.

"Tara Dalton Sanford is also your sister."

"Guilty."

"My, such talent running in your family, not to mention powerful racing connections. One married to Roberto Castillo, the other to Adam Sanford."

Tammy raised an eyebrow as she surveyed Emma-Lee's outfit that consisted of jeans and a white polo shirt emblazoned with Double S Racing. "Are you married to one of the drivers here?"

"Nope." Emma-Lee ratcheted her smile up a notch.

"Ms. Dalton." Holt's low voice sent a delicious shiver up her spine.

Emma-Lee spun around in relief. "Mr. Forrester. Have you met Mrs. Ray? Her husband's company sponsors the No. 515 team."

"Tammy, please." She extended her ring-encrusted hand.

When Holt took it, she latched on to him like a barracuda. With amusement, Emma-Lee watched as he struggled to let go.

"Your driver's Ben Edmonds?" So Holt had done his homework before coming to the race.

"For the moment."

Emma-Lee didn't miss the icy implication. It was no secret the veteran driver was not having a good season. What was hush-hush at Double S was that several sponsors were getting restless.

Holt gave the woman a wink as if they were conspirators. "Excellent. Edmonds is one of the drivers I follow. I so prefer experience over flash. Ms. Dalton, if I might see you in private about a few questions?"

He cupped her elbow and steered her away. When she saw he was making a beeline toward the entrance, she halted.

"Holt, I can't leave here. It's almost race time. I need to clear the garage of all the spectators."

"Are you going to leave me to fend for myself out there?"

Out of the corner of her eye she spotted an intense-looking driver entering the garage. Rafael O'Bryan. She'd been trying to corner him all week since Gil had given her the task of co-ordinating Rafael's interview with *Sports Scene* magazine.

"I'll be right back."

She rushed after the man. "Rafael, wait up a minute."

The elusive Double S driver looked over his shoulder, scowled and disappeared into a huddle with his crew chief and pit crew. She knew better than to interrupt the pair this close to race time. Chuckles came from another team member standing nearby.

"Better luck next time, Emma-Lee," he called out.

She gave a wave. Deflated, she returned to Holt only to have him snag her wrist.

"Who was that you were chasing after?" Despite the mildness of his tone, a tendon flexed along his jaw.

She rolled her eyes. "Rafael O'Bryan. He drives for Double S. Gil wants me to line up interviews for him except the arrogant jerk won't cooperate."

Holt's grip eased and she slipped her hand free.

"I don't get it. I thought doing interviews was part and parcel of being a NASCAR driver."

"It is. But I'm new and he keeps avoiding me."

"Emma-Lee." A tall, attractive woman approached, followed by a powerfully built man. Both bore a family resemblance, from the dark brown hair to the blue eyes. They also wore a patina of class and wealth.

"Holt…Mr. Forrester, I would like to introduce Marley Sizemore, who's in charge of sponsor relations, and Gil Sizemore, who owns Double S Racing."

Holt shook hands with Gil, whose eyes glinted with curiosity. "Holt Forrester as in HF Enterprises?"

"Yes."

"I haven't seen you around the tracks before."

Holt shrugged. "After NASCAR's and Double S's generous donations and support of the fundraiser for breast cancer last weekend, I wanted to experience a race for myself. You have quite a fan-based operation."

"Yes, we do. I hope Emma-Lee's given you a good tour of the garage. If you like what you see, perhaps we'll be able to interest you in a sponsorship."

Emma-Lee started. When Gil had asked her how the cancer event had gone, she had given him only a general overview, emphasizing the turnout so Double S would contribute again next year. Only in a nonchalant manner had she requested a pass for Holt.

Leave it to the savvy Sizemores to recognize potential

sponsors. She hadn't even considered the possibility. She sighed. She had a lot to learn about the racing business.

Marley extended a card to him. "Mr. Forrester, here's my card if you have any questions. We need to clear the garage now, but you are perfectly welcome to watch the race from our suite."

If Emma-Lee hadn't been watching his face closely, she would have missed the bemused expression in his eyes as he took the card. What on earth was going on in his mind?

However, he gave Marley a polite smile. "Thank you, maybe I'll take you up on your offer."

Emma-Lee felt a tinge of disappointment. After she finished with escorting people out, she would be joining her parents in the stands rather than going to the suite.

"First, though, I wondered if I could impose on Ms. Dalton to show me around outside. I didn't get a chance to absorb much about the track itself."

Gil laughed. "Be careful what you ask for, Holt. If anyone knows about every fact under the sun, it's Emma-Lee."

"Come on then." Chagrined, she made a sharp turn. Straight into the path of a tool cart being wheeled by a team member.

Holt's arm shot out, circled her waist and lifted her out of harm's way.

"Nice reflexes," Sizemore commented as he and his sister moved toward their cars.

"Thank you."

Emma-Lee tugged her top into place and this time turned with more caution. She hurried out of the garage with Holt following at a more leisurely pace.

Outside the stadium, lights glowed bright against the deepening blue of the late-afternoon sky. Once they had exited the secured area, she paused. "I need to speak with security. If you wait right here, I'll be back."

It didn't take her long to accomplish the task and head back to where she had left Holt. As she dodged a group of high-fiving men, she spotted Holt kneeling on the ground to pick up a bag for a middle-aged woman who was giving him her megawatt smile as only she could.

In a crowd of thousands, what were the odds?

"Mom!" Emma-Lee rushed toward them.

"Hi, honey!" Her mother offered her check for Emma-Lee's kiss. "Can you believe this nice young man has never been to a Sprint Cup Series race before? I told him he was in for a real treat with this being a short track."

Her mother winked at Holt. "I just love the way all the cameras going off in the stands twinkle like Christmas lights, don't you?"

He grinned. "Yes, ma'am."

Emma-Lee looked at him and then her mother. "How did you two meet…" Her voice trailing off, her cheeks warmed.

Eyes narrowed, her mother gave Holt her full attention. "Excuse my daughter's poor manners. I'm Shirley Dalton."

With an amused expression, he extended the bag he held. "I'm Holt Forrester. I know where Emma-Lee got her pretty looks."

"Flattery may not get you everywhere, Mr. Forrester, but compliments certainly never hurt."

"Please, call me Holt."

"Mom." Hoping to change the direction of the conversation, Emma-Lee grabbed the bag away from her and looked inside it.

"What are you doing buying more souvenirs? You already have a room filled at home."

"Not with Double S drivers. We're sadly lacking in that department. Now that you're working for Mr. Sizemore, I thought I would pick up a few things."

Shirley rummaged in the larger bag. "I have cup holders

for both Ben Edmonds and Rafael O'Bryan, Linc Shepherd's hat and an autographed photo of Eli Ward."

She shot a meaningful glance at Holt. "At the moment I'm partial to gorgeous blond hunks."

In a desperate move, Emma-Lee thrust the bag at her mother. "Mom, gotta go. See you in the stands. I'm showing Mr. Forrester around the track. It's almost race time."

Shirley kissed her daughter. "All right, honey."

Emma-Lee grabbed Holt's arm and tugged.

"Nice meeting you, Mrs. Dalton," Holt called over his shoulder.

After she led the way for a few feet, he reached out and clasped her hand. "I like your mother."

Once more the flesh-to-flesh connection sent a tingling sensation racing through her. Puzzled, Emma-Lee stared at their linked fingers. What was it with this man that was so different than when she had held other men's hands?

"My parents are cool. They've given me a good foundation. It's my fault that I haven't done anything with my life."

Oh, great, why had she blurted that out? She didn't ever discuss her insecurities. Not even her family knew.

"That's nonsense."

"Is it?" Doubt filled her. The encounter with Tammy Ray had left her edgy. "As was so recently pointed out to me in the garage, one sister is on her way to being an acclaimed actress, the other a noted journalist and author.

"And what have I accomplished so far? I lasted three weeks pursuing a career as a rock singer. I switched majors in college from geology to anthropology to history to—"

Horrified by her intensity, she stopped. *Too much information again, Emma-Lee,* she warned herself.

With a shrug, she continued in a more casual tone. "At last count I was studying to be a veterinarian. I do love animals and watching them in their natural habitat.

"There I go again," she groaned. "Many say that I don't know what I want to be when I grow up."

"Do they? Or is that what you think?" Holt raised her hand and kissed her fingertips.

"I would say that you were experiencing life and all its opportunities to its fullest, so that when you do find your avocation, you will bring to it knowledge, experience and no regrets."

Stunned by his perception, she stared at him. "Holt—"

The magic call came over the loudspeaker system. "Gentlemen, start your engines!"

Even from where they stood, the ground vibrated beneath her feet as the engines roared to life. The people in the stands erupted in a thunderous shout.

How could she not experience the excitement? How could she not be so moved that she had to throw her arms around his neck and kiss him?

To heck with caution.

SENSATIONS RUSHED through Holt like he'd been thrust into a free-fall dive without a chute.

Everything around him blurred until there was only Emma-Lee. When her mouth softened under his, longing, unexpected as it was fierce and intense, clawed his insides.

At the back of his mind a dim alarm sounded, but he ignored it as he cupped the back of her neck. The kiss sizzled, smoldered and sparked. He needed more. He slanted his mouth to take the kiss deeper.

"Hey, buddy, get a room!"

The ribald laughter penetrated the sensual haze, and he lifted his head. Around them race-goers gave them knowing smiles.

Holt tensed. What the hell had happened to his control? He'd been making out in public like a teenager with raging hormones. He gripped Emma-Lee's wrists and stepped clear of her embrace.

She let her arms fall to her sides as she stood looking up at him. Confusion and uncertainty flickered in her eyes.

Talk about screwing things up. That's what he got for losing his much-vaunted control.

"Emma-Lee, I'm sorry. I'm attracted to you, but kissing a woman in public..." In frustration he raked his fingers through his hair. He wasn't used to explaining himself.

To his surprise she reached out and took his hand. "Holt, it's okay. Let's just write off the moment due to the thrill of the race."

Okay. Swell. She wasn't reading anything into the kiss. Why did that thought depress him?

She released his hand and stepped away. Her smile wobbled at the edges before firming. "I need to find my folks. However, they always cook dinner after the race. I know Mom would want me to invite you. You can't miss the cherry-red mobile home in the lot, as most people will hightail it out of here after the race."

Dinner...with the folks? Oh, no. Too much. Too family for him.

Case in point. When he'd returned his father's phone call last Sunday night, there had been long gaps of dead air. Whatever renewed connection the fundraiser had generated between them had already run its course. Much as he liked her mother, having a meal with Emma-Lee's folks would be ten times more awkward.

He shook his head. "I think I will drop into Sizemore's suite for a while and then head to the airport. I'm in the process of launching a new software line and have meetings in Atlanta all this week."

"Of course. I'll show you to the sponsor suite."

"No, I've taken enough of your time. Marley wrote the

number on the back of this card, so I can find it on my own. Go enjoy the race."

"All right. Well." She held out her hand. "It was nice seeing you again, Holt."

For some inexplicable reason the civil pleasantry irritated him. "Emma-Lee." He ignored her hand and gave her a quick, hard kiss. "You take care."

He stalked off, leaving her with a bewildered expression. Make that two, he thought. Why on earth was he heading toward a room with people he didn't know when he could be with Emma-Lee?

Because business was business. He grimaced. Besides, given the way Emma-Lee intrigued him, he should retreat until he had this fascination firmly under control. Stay within his well-defined world. Safer that way.

An hour later Holt held a glass of water and considered bolting to the airport. It wasn't as if the Sizemores weren't gracious hosts, for they were. Both Gil and Marley had engaged in the polite dance of courting. They wanted something from him, and he wanted something from them.

A fair business exchange from which he had garnered important information about the racing industry. The other sponsors' gossip was worth its weight in gold.

However, he was peopled out. Time to retreat to his Atlanta hotel room that currently served as home. He set down his glass and approached Gil to say his goodbyes. Gil held up a finger as he unclipped his vibrating cell phone.

"Yes, Emma-Lee?"

Holt stilled and strained to hear her voice.

"Of course. Don't worry about tonight. I hope your friend feels better."

Gil disconnected and returned the phone to his belt.

Holt couldn't help himself. "Is everything all right?"

Gil shook his head. "Emma-Lee has a friend undergoing

chemotherapy. She had a bad session yesterday so Emma-Lee's flying to Charlotte to be with her."

"Excuse me, Gil." Turning away, Holt pulled out his phone and called Emma-Lee. "Meet me out front," he said without preamble. "I have a jet at the airport that can be ready by the time we get there."

He heard her hiss of breath. "But, Holt, I can't ask you to—"

"It's not a problem." He hung up and turned back to the other man.

"Thank you for your hospitality, Gil."

The race owner gave him an appraising stare before he nodded. "You're welcome. You take care of *our* Emma-Lee."

Holt didn't miss the thinly veiled warning, but he turned and left the suite.

He had bigger demons to contend with. Emma-Lee needed his help.

But in order to help her he would have to confront his own private hell. However, he recalled only too vividly the effects of chemotherapy on his mother. He didn't want Emma-Lee to face it by herself. Whenever a disease took up residence, it liked to kick in the teeth of all who dared to come near.

CHAPTER FIVE

THE LIGHT ILLUMINATING the spacious front porch of the neat colonial-style house barely held the night's darkness at bay.

Emma-Lee cast a worried glance at Holt as they crossed the sidewalk from the driveway. On the short flight from Richmond to Charlotte the few stabs she had taken at conversation had fizzled. The jet had both intrigued and bothered her at the same time. Once she had learned it was his, she had immediately asked why he hadn't used it in West Virginia. His explanation—in for repairs—had been simple but terse, leaving her to wonder if there was more to the matter.

Yet when she had started to talk about her friend Sandy, he had snapped open his laptop and indicated he needed to review a report.

The closer they had gotten to Charlotte, the more remote his expression had become. He'd bundled her into the sleek black sedan waiting for them at the airport, asked for the address and directions and hadn't said a word since then.

Had he regretted his decision to come with her? She stopped on the sidewalk. "Holt, I can't thank you enough for getting me here, but you don't have to go in. This isn't your problem. Sandy will put me up for the night. I'll be fine."

"Don't be ridiculous." He took her elbow and propelled her up the wide steps.

The door swung open and Jeffrey Colton stood in the entry. She sucked in a breath. A sports attorney at a major law firm, Jeff normally epitomized the professional image with pressed pants and crisp, long-sleeved shirts. Tonight with rumbled clothes, five-o'clock shadow and dark circles under his eyes, he looked more like a college student who had pulled one too many all-nighters.

"Jeff." She rushed forward and kissed him on the cheek. "Where's Sandy?"

"In our bedroom with the door locked. We had a fight earlier. I guess that's when she called you."

Jeff seemed to notice Holt for the first time. "Sorry. Forgive the manners. I'm Jeff Colton."

"Holt Forrester." They shook hands and Jeff stood aside so they could enter. She turned left into the disaster area that was the living room. Emma-Lee's stomach twisted. Dear God, Sandy was such a neat freak.

"Jeff." She gestured.

"Sorry." He bent to pick pages of newspaper tossed on the floor. "Sandy's had no energy, and I've been working late hours on a major deal for a client."

"I had no idea," she murmured. *But you should have thought of it last weekend and asked if they needed help. You knew how tired Sandy had been in college during treatment.*

"Em-a-e!" In the middle of the large sofa, the couple's thirteen-month-old daughter whose reddened eyes told of a recent crying jag held up her arms.

"Hi, sweetheart!" Emma-Lee picked her up and cuddled the toddler close. She inhaled the wonderful scent of powder and baby. There was nothing sweeter.

Over the child's tousled red curls, she smiled at Holt. "Emily Rose, I want you to meet my friend Holt."

The child gave him a tearful look and then hid her face in the crook of Emma-Lee's shoulder.

"Sorry, she's a little cranky—" Jeff stopped and scrubbed his face with both hands. "God. It seems like all I ever do anymore is apologize."

He lowered his hands. "My wife had a bad chemo session and has been throwing up all weekend. She's—"

"*She* is standing here and would appreciate it if people quit speaking as if *she* was already gone."

Emma-Lee turned. Pale and gaunt, her friend stood by the sofa, hanging on to it with both hands. She wore a bright, patterned silk scarf tied around her head. One only had to look at the family photos lining the fireplace mantel on the other side of the room to know mother and daughter shared the same red-gold hair.

"Here." Emma-Lee thrust the child into the arms of the very startled Holt. She hurried around the sofa.

"Hi, Sandy. Let's go have girl talk and let the boys watch the race if it's still on."

She circled an arm around her friend's waist, but Sandy kept a death grip on the sofa. "Nice to meet you in person, Holt. I was disappointed when you didn't come over with Emma-Lee last Sunday."

"Sorry, but I had a business meeting." He glanced up from watching with horrified fascination the child sniffing his leather jacket. The girl also lifted her head, leaving a spot of drool on the leather.

"How are you, Sandy?" His serious eyes were intent.

Her friend gave a weak laugh. "I've had better moments. I think Jeff could use some male companionship."

She released her hold and linked her arm with Emma-Lee's. They went into the blue-and-ivory master bedroom where the stink of sickness filled the air.

"Let's get some fresh air in here."

Emma-Lee guided her friend to the over-scaled chair covered with blue tapestry fabric in the far corner. Then she went to the windows and drew them up a few inches. Looking around, she spotted a throw tossed on the bed and picked it up. She returned to the chair and wrapped the blanket around Sandy's shoulders.

"Scoot over," she ordered. When Sandy obliged, Emma-Lee sat next to her and tugged an end of the throw around her. Sandy's body was as stiff as a board. She reached out and held her friend's hand.

"I like your Holt."

"So do I, but…"

"But what?"

Could she really put a finger on what had happened at the Richmond track when he had visibly withdrawn into a shell and then bolted after she kissed him?

A kiss that even as she remembered it still sent a quiver through her. A man whose kiss was that potent…was she getting in over her head?

Emma-Lee lifted a shoulder. "At times I feel like he's on one side of a computer monitor viewing the rest of the world through it. He said something when we first met that makes me think he avoids any type of emotional commitment."

Sandy snorted. "Girlfriend, he brought you here, didn't he?"

"Yes, but—"

"It's not like you to be so cautious." Sandy flipped her hand over and gripped hers in return. "Normally you're more reckless, going where others fear to tread, a quality I've always rather envied."

"Me? I've always been jealous of you."

"Old stick-in-the-mud Sandy Colton? Come on."

"You're a teacher, married to a fabulous man, and have a gorgeous child."

"Oh, that's right." Sandy snapped her fingers. "You should be envious." The tension in her body eased as she laughed and rested her head on Emma-Lee's shoulder.

"What happened this weekend, Sandy?"

"Oh, nothing other than my going on a self-pity binge. My oncologist was cautiously optimistic on Friday and said I need only two more treatments for now."

"Honey, that's wonderful." Emma-Lee kissed her cheek.

"Yeah, you would think I'd be in a better mood, wouldn't you?" She sighed.

"But when I got home, Jeff treated me like I was made of fragile glass and I kept vomiting. Hardly the stuff that would get a man into a romantic mood. Then you called all excited about BASE jumping and meeting Mr. Amazing out there."

"Oh, Sandy, I didn't mean to upset you."

Her friend shook their clasped hands. "I know that. I just wish…"

"What?"

Sandy lifted her head and looked at her with tear-filled eyes. "I wish people wouldn't be so afraid that if they touch me then they would get sick, as well. Cancer's not contagious, it's only a personal albatross."

Like an internal savage blush a wave of shame raced through Emma-Lee. How many times had she wanted to escape her friend's illness? How many times had she been afraid the cancer would reach out and grab her?

Her throat was so tight that she croaked, "Confession time?"

"You at times are scared of getting it?"

Oh, God. Sandy knew? Emma-Lee inhaled sharply. "That obvious?"

"Only on occasion. At least you're been there for me even if you secretly wanted to bolt. Several friends have dropped off the face of the planet."

She swallowed—hard—to speak past the growing lump in her throat. "Sorry. At times I feel so guilty that I'm healthy and you're not."

Sandy pursed her lips. "I have days where I hate you because you're brimming with life."

At first the confession astounded Emma-Lee, but then relief seeped in. She wasn't alone in being less than perfect.

"Guilt and hate. Don't we make a wonderful team?"

"It makes us human, Emma-Lee. But you forgot to add love and respect to our dynamic."

She sought comfort through the ritual the pair had begun in college when they had their first fight. She twisted her hand until her small finger hooked the similar finger on Sandy's hand.

"Still friends?"

"Friends forever." Sandy sighed and let her hand drop. "So tired."

"Close your eyes for a moment and rest."

As she heard her friend's breathing even out, Emma-Lee stretched out her legs. So long as they could push past the fear of death, they would be all right. They had to be. Weary, she shut her eyes.

"I FIGURE YOU OWE ME a debt of gratitude." Jeff tucked the blanket around Emily Rose sleeping peacefully in the crib.

Holt still trying to figure out how the heck he'd ended up in as unlikely a place as a child's nursery on a Saturday night gave the other man a blank look. "What?"

The father turned on a night-light and picked up a few stuffed animals from the floor. "When I first met Sandy, she was glued to the hip with Emma-Lee. You would have thought they were blood twins rather than college roommates. Many a guy tried and failed to get past one's scrutiny in order to date the other."

He placed the toys in a painted wood cabinet. "It took quite a bit of clever and skilled maneuvering by me to separate Sandy from her anchor."

Despite the little voice in his head warning him he was getting too involved, Holt was fascinated. "Emma-Lee's the anchor of their friendship?"

Jeff threw him a puzzled glance. "Haven't you been drawn into her fold by now? She comes from such a tight-knit family that she radiates this warmth and openness. Sandy's folks divorced when she was young and she got kicked to the side. Enter Emma-Lee with her open arms and heart and presto, a friendship as thick as blood.

"By convincing Emma-Lee that I was Mr. Right for Sandy, I was able to win Sandy's heart."

He moved past Holt into the hallway. "Given my wife's ad nauseam conversation this week of how you rescued Emma-Lee, you've come a long way in securing her approval. You may even stand a chance with Emma-Lee where others have failed."

Holt slipped his hands into his pockets. "I'll have to remember that detail."

He should make an excuse and leave. It wasn't as if Emma-Lee was expecting him to stay. The women had been hidden away in the bedroom for an hour now without a sign of them reappearing. For all he knew, Emma-Lee had forgotten he was even here.

Up until now, he'd been unable to offer anything but a pat on the shoulder or a brief comment when others faced illness or death. Another indication Emma-Lee was starting to mean something more to him. Watching his mother's long and ultimately unsuccessful fight with cancer had burned out all ability to deal with any more sickness. He'd borne the burden once in life, and he didn't intend to ever go through such an ordeal again. The pain at the end was simply too agonizing to bear.

Jeff stopped in front of the bedroom door and silently

turned the handle. The tender expression that swept across his face was so private Holt had to turn his head.

"Come here. You have to see this."

With leaden feet, Holt approached the door and looked inside. Across the room the two women slept peacefully together in a chair. Emma-Lee's arm was wrapped protectively around her friend's shoulders.

An emotion so raw and alien to him that he couldn't even label it gripped his heart. He rubbed the heel of his hand over his chest to relieve the ache.

The scene before him tore loose a memory. Right after his mother had been diagnosed, her crying had awakened him. He'd run into his parents' bedroom. His father had been holding her, running a comforting hand along her back. Unable to bear the look of grief on his father's face, Holt had backed out without saying anything.

Holt retreated, from the memory, from the Coltons' bedroom.

Swinging the door closed, Jeff whispered, "Beautiful, aren't they?"

"Yes." The question burst from Holt. "How do you bear it?"

"Sandy's illness?"

"Yes."

Jeff lowered his head. "I could give you the easy answer that I made a vow to be with her in sickness and health." He waved his hand. "But you and I both know how easily that pledge is broken in this day and age.

"I bear it because my life began and will end with Sandy. She's everything. Together we will beat the cancer. Together we will watch Emily Rose grow up and, God willing, have several more kids."

To Holt's consternation, Jeff's shoulders shook and he pressed a hand to his eyes.

"Excuse me." The man hurried down the hall and disappeared inside the bathroom.

Holt leaned against the wall. Emotionally, his father hadn't survived the loss of his wife. Leaving Holt to fend for himself with his grief, Sam Forrester had retreated into the black-and-white world of mathematics he taught at the local college. No family member or friend had stepped forward to help.

The Coltons were very fortunate. They had Emma-Lee in their corner.

CHAPTER SIX

EARLY-MORNING STILLNESS filled the house as Emma-Lee stole down the hallway to the guest bathroom. Inside she turned on the shower. Once undressed, she stepped under the spray and heaved a sigh of relief as pelting drops of hot water eased muscles stiff from spending a night in the chair.

She lifted her face to the spray. Last night's heart-to-heart talk with Sandy had scrubbed her emotionally clean, but she still was a little raw around the edges. Before leaving Sandy, she had given her friend a hug and then held on longer than she should have, willing her health into her friend's fragile body.

Stop it. Emma-Lee gave the tap a sharp twist, grabbed a towel and dried off. For now she had to be strong for Sandy. What they all needed was a good breakfast. Even her pathetic culinary skills ought to be able to conjure something up in the kitchen.

She pulled on a pair of yoga pants and then a T-shirt she'd borrowed from Sandy. As her friend had dropped a couple sizes due to her latest round of chemotherapy, the shirt fit way too snug. Emma-Lee ran her hands under the white fabric to stretch it. The outfit would have to do until she got home.

However she got home, since Holt had probably left last night.

Not that she could blame him. After all, he had ridden to her rescue, only to land smack-dab in another family's crisis. Given the mess of her own emotions in dealing with cancer striking someone close to her, how had he as a boy handled the death of his mother? Had the loss driven him to fear any emotional connections to others?

She couldn't fathom a life without family and friends. Family loved you for yourself, no matter how much you screwed up, and provided a frame. Friends were trickier, but she loved discovering how the person's life experiences molded the individual. She could thread their perspectives with hers.

But a soul mate would bring...

The pang of longing that welled deep inside shocked her. She braced her hands on the edge of the sink, stared into the misted mirror and examined the stunned expression on her image's face.

"Emma-Lee Dalton, are you out of your ever-loving mind?" she whispered. "When did you add settling down with Mr. Perfect to the list of things you need to change about your life? Don't you think you have enough on your plate just figuring out who you are and a career you can stick to for more than five minutes?"

The woman in the mirror had no response other than to shake her head. Figured.

Emma-Lee turned in exasperation, bent and scooped up her clothes. Finding a good man like her father, her brothers-in-law or Jeff was a huge order. Huge.

Who was she kidding? If she didn't know herself, how could she add a man to the mix?

She went out into the hall. Sandy and Jeff's bedroom door was closed. As she paused by it, she heard the low sound of Jeff's laughter and Sandy's responding giggle. Looking upward, she whispered a quick prayer of thanks.

She'd better check on Emily Rose and see if she was awake. She could at least manage the toddler's breakfast and watch her. Emma-Lee stepped inside the child's room, but the crib was empty. Concerned, she hurried on to the living room and dumped her clothes on the sofa beside a neatly folded blanket and pillow. Where was the baby?

She heard the gurgle of young laughter at the same time the rich aroma of coffee reached her nose. Of course. Emily Rose was in the playpen set up in the kitchen. Jeff must have put a pot on before going in to see Sandy. Her system could use a caffeine boost.

Emma-Lee wandered into the kitchen and halted, transfixed by the scene before her. In a high-top chair by the built-in banquet, Emily Rose scooped up a dripping spoonful of colorful cereal loops, crammed them into her mouth and then munched contentedly. Holt, wearing a black T-shirt and jeans, stood barefoot by the stainless-steel range. With competent movements, he cracked several eggs into a skillet.

Yearning raced through her and ran right over her heart.

Oh, no. Since her legs suddenly had all the consistency of jelly, she leaned against the doorjamb. How could she switch gears so quickly from arguing against finding the perfect man to this?

Her heart held up the simple answer: she wanted—no, needed—this man with all his sharp edges and complications.

She exhaled deeply, releasing the breath she had not been aware she was holding.

Holt glanced up and as he gave her a slow survey, his eyes heated. "Nice outfit. I hope you like eggs and bacon."

"Love them." Make nothing of the fact he's here. Act as if a gorgeous man cooking for you in the morning is a regular thing.

She crossed the room and kissed Emily Rose's cereal-crusted cheek. "That's a Dalton traditional weekend breakfast along with Dad's homemade pancakes and maple syrup."

Holt peeled off thick strips of bacon and dropped them in another large skillet. His brows knitted together as he checked the eggs. "The only pancakes I can make are the prepared-batter kind."

Emma-Lee grabbed silverware from a drawer and set the table with them along with napkins. "You're ahead of the game on me. I merely pop the frozen ones in the toaster oven."

After checking Emily Rose's cuppie, she grabbed a container of apple juice from the fridge and placed it on the table. She next opened a cupboard, removed plates and placed them on the counter next to Holt. She then leaned against the counter. "Do you like to cook?"

He shot her a startled glance before grabbing tongs from the utensil holder. "Like?" He mulled over the word as he turned the strips of bacon.

"Cooking was more a matter of survival when I was a kid. My only other option was to eat in the cafeteria on the college campus where my father taught. The moment I could afford to eat in restaurants I abandoned any culinary skills I might have had."

No time like the present to cross Holt's invisible No Trespassing sign she'd sensed about his personal life. "Your father didn't cook?"

The kitchen's cozy environment must have lowered his usual reserve, for Holt hesitated only a fraction of a second before answering.

"Dad didn't do much of anything after Mom died other than retreat into his lessons and the never-ending book he was writing about his mathematical theories."

The neutral tone of his voice didn't quite conceal the note of bitterness. Emma-Lee thought of her family and how they were always there for her. Instead of the man before her, she suddenly saw a lonely boy making his own meal. Sadness mixed with compassion welled up in her.

"That must have been rough."

He shrugged off the comment. "I survived."

He removed the crisp bacon and laid the strips on a paper towel. "Plates, please."

She handed him one and he piled on a generous serving of eggs and bacon. "Hey, leave some for Jeff and Sandy!"

Amusement sparkled in his eyes. "Jeff told me I was on my own for breakfast and entrusted me with Emily Rose under penalty of death. I had to prove I knew how to pick up and hold her before he went to check on Sandy. He looked like a man on a mission."

"Oh." Remembering the laughter from the bedroom, Emma-Lee smiled and handed him the second plate.

After he heaped on the rest of the eggs, he followed her to the banquet and sat across the table. They dug into the food. Beside them the toddler sipped from her cuppie. After a few minutes of companionable silence, she dared to continue the topic of his family.

"Is your father still teaching?"

"Yes." Holt drank some of his coffee.

She forked a bite of egg. When Emily Rose opened her mouth expectantly, she smiled. "Here you go, sugar." She fed the toddler several more bites before asking, "Did your father ever finish his book?"

"Yes." Holt's mouth twisted. "And before you ask, the small press at the university where he works did publish it. In the sterile world of his contemporaries the book did well. But you won't find it at any commercial bookstore."

Her face heated and she laid down her fork. "I didn't mean to pry."

"Sure you did. You're inquisitive about people. It's what makes you who you are."

The rough edge to his voice suggested that he didn't necessarily think curiosity was such a good trait. More than a table separated them. Their view of how to relate to others gaped before her.

The toddler banged her cuppie and raised her plump fist. "Em-a-lee. More juice." Emma-Lee grabbed the cup before it went flying, twisted off the top and poured in more juice. After securing the top, she handed the cup to the toddler. All the while she puzzled over her growing feelings for Holt.

How could you care about another if you didn't know them beyond the surface presented to the world? Still, the image of the young Holt abandoned in his time of emotional need disturbed her.

She reached across the table to touch his hand. "For what it's worth, I'm sure your father is very proud of you and what you've done in honor of your mother's memory."

Holt caught her fingers before she could withdraw. The link sent a jolt through her with tension coiling in her stomach. Could he not feel the connection?

He squeezed gently, just enough to convey a warning. "Emma-Lee, I'm not one of those people you can collect and fix. Dad chose his path a long time ago, and I made do with mine."

He turned her hand over and studied the lines as if he was trying to read her future. "Forget about my parents, my past. I want to know if you think there's something happening between us?"

She stood on the precarious edge of the chasm of vulnerability. To declare one's sentiments without a safety net of knowing if the other person felt the same way. The leap of faith.

Emma-Lee took a deep breath and dived off that tenuous span.

She curled her fingers around his. "Yes, Holt."

Briefly, he closed his eyes, but when he reopened them, a volatile mix of relief and desire burned in them. Tension radiated from him as he leaned across the table. She met him halfway.

His mouth settled on hers, soft and warm. The unexpected gentleness of the kiss tied her system into knots. He rose, bringing her up with him. He moved around the table and circled his arm around her waist, drawing her close against the hard lines of his body, even as he took his mouth on a leisurely journey over her face. Her eyes drifted half-closed. When he rained kisses across her temple, her heart took a slow spin.

Something trembled inside her, fragile as a rosebud about to bloom. Overwhelmed, she clung to his broad shoulders. He raised his head for a second, his smile slow and all too knowing. He ran a questing hand along the curve of her spine until he found the exposed flesh between the shirt and pants. She shuddered as the contact branded her.

When he returned to her lips, the hunger in his kiss sent her sinking deep, deeper still into a stormy haze where raw needs sparked and threatened to flare.

The dim banging sound of plastic striking plastic penetrated the sensual fog that enveloped Emma-Lee. She opened her eyes and saw as if from a distance sunlight pouring through the kitchen window. The Coltons' kitchen window.

She tensed. What was she doing? Free-falling into a firestorm of passion? She wasn't prepared for that particular jump, at least not yet.

Holt stilled and raised his head. His eyes were serious and veiled as if he had already withdrawn behind his protective wall. "What's wrong?"

She licked her swollen lips, tasting him. She would never forget his flavor as long as she lived.

"I'm sorry." Her voice came out as a half croak. She swallowed and tried again. "This is the wrong time, the wrong—"

"Wrong man?" Although his voice was flat, she heard the edge of vulnerability behind the question.

"No." She shook her head. "The wrong place."

As if on cue, the toddler stopping hitting the cuppie on the tray and raised her arms. "Em-a-lee. Down. I want down."

Holt released her and she stepped away. She picked up the girl, carried her over to the playpen in the corner by the refrigerator, and placed her inside. From a nearby hamper overflowing with toys, she selected a few favorites and placed in the playpen a battered teddy bear, a set of stacking plastic rings and pop beads. The reprieve of the routine gave her a few moments to steady herself.

She turned and caught Holt studying her with a stunned expression. Within the blink of an eye, though, his face resumed its usual enigmatic mask. Definitely, she wasn't the only one thrown off balance by the kiss. Still, what did one say following a mind-blowing kiss? Shrug it off, she decided.

"I know you need to get back to Atlanta, if you want to leave. Mooresville is only a short drive from here. I can get a lift from Jeff."

He paced toward her like a stalking panther. She backed up until she bumped into the fridge. Its gentle humming matched that of the pulsing of her blood. He halted and gently cupped her chin, forcing her eyes to meet his.

"Emma-Lee?"

She swallowed—hard. "Yes, Holt?"

"That wasn't a kiss caused by situational hormones." He lightly brushed his lips against hers.

She almost sagged against him, but she managed to whisper, "It wasn't?"

"No." He sighed and pressed his forehead against hers. "I can't promise you anything, but I only know that I have to see you again. I have meetings all week in Atlanta, but I can free up time next weekend."

She shook her head. "I'll be in Darlington for the race."

"Can you dig up another pass for me?"

"Sure." Disappointment mixed with relief. A whole week before she saw him again. Time enough to get her head straight without the dizzying influence of his presence.

He lifted his head and stared out the window. "It's a nice day." Light gleamed in his eyes. "Why don't we say our good-byes to the Coltons and I'll drive you home."

HOLDING TWO HELMETS, Holt stood waiting in the driveway as Emma-Lee kissed and hugged Sandy at the door. She hadn't spotted his surprise yet. Anticipation unfurled inside him. She turned, took one step down from the portico and halted. Her eyes widened and then her smile bloomed.

The sunny day couldn't compete with the warmth of her expression. He knew he would do about anything to keep that smile on her face. All the last-minute scrambling had been worth it even if it had meant rousting Ted on a Sunday morning.

Satisfied, he waited as she hurried down the walk to the driveway.

"Oh, man." Her voice was reverential. He stepped aside so she could check out the gleaming black-and-chrome monster of a motorcycle.

"But how, when? We drove here in a car last night." She trailed a finger along the fender.

"While you were taking your sweet time getting ready—"

"I was not getting ready." Emma-Lee crossed her arms and tapped her foot. "Sandy needed to speak with me."

"Anyway, while Jeff and I were twiddling our thumbs, I called Ted and had him bring the bike in exchange for the car. I thought it was too nice a day to spend riding cooped up in a car."

With that he thrust one of the helmets toward her. Grinning, she put on the helmet and cinched the strap. Holt straddled the bike and held out his hand. She climbed on. He kicked up the stand, turned on the engine, and with a roar of pure power, sped down the driveway.

The cool morning air contrasted with the warmth of Emma-Lee's body pressed against his. Buildings whipped by as Holt drove through Charlotte. Soon they were on the interstate cutting through the rolling countryside. The bike answered his call for more speed and surged forward.

Tomorrow he would wonder why his whole life had shifted in the kitchen when he had seen Emma-Lee with the toddler and had wanted it all. In the sanctuary of his room he would analyze why his clear-cut plans now revolved around having a family.

With the wind in his face, he let his mind empty of all thought, uncertainties and memories. There was only the now. The blue sky above, the powerful motorcycle beneath, the gorgeous woman behind and the shimmering highway before him.

When Emma-Lee removed her hands from his shoulders, he turned his head slightly. She threw up her arms and laughed with sheer pleasure.

Then she wrapped her arms around his waist, pressing even closer to him until they were one and shouted, "Faster!"

He covered her hands with his and knew he would always remember this moment. Then he leaned forward and gunned the motor.

CHAPTER SEVEN

PENSIVELY, HOLT LOOKED OUT at the once carefully mapped formula of his life. The vision of Emma-Lee holding the toddler on Sunday had thrown new data into the equation, irrevocably changing him. If he was being brutally honest with himself, his life had changed from the moment he had caught her at the New River Gorge.

His concession came Wednesday as around him his marketing team continued their projections of the expected sales of his new computer game.

Seated in the conference room for the Atlanta office of HF Enterprises' latest venture, he gazed broodingly into the sleek laptop's screen as if it were a crystal ball, searching for answers that his computer for once couldn't give.

He'd spent most of his life in the painless, clear world of computerized data. There was no past or future, only the present for him to deal with black-and-white facts and figures.

However, now instead of numbers he saw only the image of Emma-Lee's smile. Rather than the game wizard's voice announcing the player had reached a new level as Holt checked the game for any flaws, he heard only her laughter.

Face it. After yet another sleepless night he knew he had it bad when he had stood on the balcony of his hotel room watching the sunrise and wishing she was with him.

He was sure she would know some fascinating fact of how daybreak in Atlanta was different than in any other city. Or recite the city's history back to prehistoric ages when some molecule changed the course of human events.

Since he had left her on the doorstep of her apartment in Mooresville, how many times had he thought of her, reached for the phone and pulled back just in time?

It wasn't like him to need to hear another's voice so much. But then again, that kiss in the Coltons' kitchen wasn't like him either....

A terrifying free fall without a parachute into an unknown void of emotional need.

Physical needs he could handle. He'd always been able to end relationships, usually on good terms, before feelings got in the way.

Look at how he had broken up with Marguerite after he had returned from the BASE jump. No regrets, no hard feelings. A clean break.

Like the character he now propelled through the game paces, Holt knew if he continued on this new course, it could only mean disaster. Emma-Lee was a woman who spelled commitment with a capital *M,* as in marriage.

What did he know about being a family, a husband or a father? Holt flexed his fingers on top of the keyboard.

After all, he had only twelve years of memories of being a family unit before his mother's death to give him any type of foundation. Wanting to be a different father than his own had been didn't mean he knew how to do it.

A person couldn't change who he was, not deep down inside. The survivor technique of using remoteness as a shield between him and the rest of the world had become his sword as an adult. How could he lower it now?

What did they have in common other than being risk-takers in sports? She had a thirst for life and a love of people. How could he correlate that with his carefully maintained universe of isolation? After two days of meetings, he was ready to escape. Maybe he should go rock climbing, skydiving or any sport that might spur his blood to race more than Emma-Lee. To prove he didn't need her.

Right. Might as well sell him some e-stock for a bridge to nowhere.

So where did that leave him? In uncharted territory, as far as his relationships were concerned. Dinner. He could take her out to dinner. He was good at taking women out to dinner. Like a drowning man grasping at a lifeline, he seized on the familiar.

Before him lights flared on the laptop's screen and the game wizard shouted with glee, "Loser, loser."

The room fell silent as everyone's jaw dropped. Never had he failed to gain the mathematician's cave and gain the secret equation to win. After all, he had invented the game. He rose and gave a rueful grin.

"Great job, everyone. I think we're ready to launch. If anyone needs anything, you know how to reach me."

He strode out of the room and checked his watch. He could arrive in Mooresville in time to take Emma-Lee out for dinner. Somewhere intimate and quiet where they wouldn't be disturbed. He nodded with satisfaction. Women like romantic settings.

Now that he had a course of action, he was anxious to implement it. Nothing more black and white in a relationship than wining and dining a woman.

A foolproof step for him to take things to the next level with Emma-Lee.

"SANDY, ARE YOU SURE that you don't want me to babysit tomorrow night?" Emma-Lee pulled her purse out of the deep bottom drawer of her desk and dumped it next to the gym bag on the floor. She'd already changed into jeans, T-shirt and sneakers.

"No, Jeff's parents will watch Emily Rose for us." Sandy's excitement infused her voice. When she had called a few minutes earlier, she'd practically screamed the news Jeff was taking her to dinner to celebrate his landing a major basketball contract for a client.

Funny how something as simple as going on a dinner date could be a major milestone in the return to normalcy in a relationship.

"I'm happy for you, honey. I'm going to want all the juicy details." She opened a desk drawer and swept an assortment of pens from the top into it. She closed the drawer.

"Speaking of details, what's going on with Holt?"

"He's coming to the race Saturday."

"And afterward, ummm?"

"He hasn't mentioned doing anything." Like he hadn't given her any affirmation of his feelings toward her on Sunday. She knew he cared for her, but it would be nice security to have the words.

"Keep me posted."

"10-4. Talk to you later, Sandy. I've got to go."

Emma-Lee disconnected.

"Hey, Emma-Lee!" The Double S receptionist, Connie, waved as she walked by. "You're going to the go-kart challenge tonight, aren't you?"

"Yes, I'll be there in a few."

Shortly after noon a frenzy of e-mails had sped through Double S headquarters. Someone had bragged about their time at the local go-kart track. Another had responded he could beat the time any day. Pretty soon it appeared that Double S employees were the all-star champions of the universe when it came to go-kart times. There was only one way to settle who was fastest, and the challenge was on for tonight. Emma-Lee had a very important bet with one of Rafael O'Bryan's team members she was determined to win.

She checked the phone display for any messages that may have come in while she was in the restroom. Nothing. Gil was holed up with the Double S crew chiefs, so she could leave. On cue the phone rang and with a groan she picked up.

"Um, Emma-Lee." Connie sounded distracted. "You have a visitor. He says he doesn't have an appointment but assured me you would see him."

"Is that right?" Sighing at the possible delay, she straightened the desk pad on top of the desk. After two days with neither a call nor an e-mail from Holt, she was more than ready to blow off some of her doldrums by bumping cars.

Since when had she ever moped over a man? She had always lived in the moment. Normally she wouldn't hesitate over calling a guy, but she'd caught a remote, shuttered expression in Holt's eyes when he'd left her Sunday after a very chaste goodbye kiss. What an anticlimax it had been to the wild motorcycle ride.

She was pretty sure the loner had gone into full retreat like a tortoise into his shell. As she wasn't sure what to do about that mind-bending, toe-tingling kiss in the kitchen, maybe she should leave well enough alone until Saturday.

"Emma-Lee, are you there?" Connie's voice snapped her back to the job at hand.

"Yes, Connie. I'm here. What is his name?"

"Holt Forrester." Connie's voice lowered and came over the line muffled. "Emma-Lee, you've been holding out on me. He's yummy!"

"I'll be right out." Emma-Lee hung up. The news that Holt was here sent her system humming with nerves. Why was he here? Why hadn't he called?

She picked up her bags and slung them over her shoulder. She hurried down from the executive suite to the front. Connie gave her a slight wink as she strolled into the reception area.

At the vision before her she halted, her breath backing up.

Holt stood in profile as he studied a poster of one of the race cars. Slanting rays of the late-afternoon sun glazed him like one of those golden Greek gods she had studied when she had been in her "going to teach mythology" stage.

He wandered to the next poster, his gaze intense as he studied it. What would it be like to have him look at her with such focus in the hush of the night or in the early hours of dawn?

He glanced over and saw her. His eyes heated up and a slow smile curved his lips.

Oh, yeah, just like that for every day for the rest of her life. She wiped her suddenly sweaty palm on her jeans and amped up a smile.

"Holt, what a surprise. Weren't you supposed to be in Atlanta all week?"

He approached her, so close she had to tilt her head up. "If you're finished here for the day—" his gaze flickered to the bags she carried before returning to her face "—I would like to take you to dinner."

A bona fide date. Hadn't she been wishing for precisely this? She opened her mouth to say yes, when she heard Connie clear her throat behind her. She gave the receptionist a glare over her shoulder, and the other woman threw up her hands. "I'm leaving, I'm leaving. See you at the challenge…or not."

However, Connie's interruption had served its purpose. Not only had Emma-Lee promised to go, but she also had a wager she needed to win.

Holt's eyebrow cocked. "Challenge?"

"We're having a friendly race with go-karts tonight. Some serious trash talking went on today about who had the fastest time." She took a deep breath. "I'm committed to do one race."

He reached out and traced the curve of her cheek. Her skin

heated from the simple touch. "Can't you skip the racing? I've already made reservations."

Meaning he had assumed she would drop everything to go out with him. She was so not going down the path where she would put her life on hold, hoping that he would come and see her. She could never respect herself, let alone expect him to respect her, if she became a doormat.

She tilted her chin. "No, I can't. I made a promise. If you had called me, I could have saved you the trouble of coming here."

His mouth thinning, Holt dropped his hand.

Guilt immediately assailed Emma-Lee. He had flown here after all. "Of course, you're welcome to come with me to the race. With all the people going it should be a blast."

"Afraid to be alone with me, Emma-Lee?" he asked quietly.

"What do you mean?"

"Every time we're together, we're surrounded by people."

There was safety in numbers, particularly when you could be in over your head. "Not everyone lives in a vacuum, Holt," she retorted.

Amusement lit his eyes. "True, but no couple can survive in a three-ring circus. Is it wrong that I want to be alone with you, to get to know you?"

"No, but you can't expect me to drop my life when it's convenient for you. What if I had come to Atlanta and interrupted one of your meetings?"

"You already did," he muttered.

"What?"

Dull red flags spread across his cheeks. Holt hitched a shoulder. "Nothing. So if I go to this challenge then you will spend time alone with me?"

Enchanted with his obvious discomfort, Emma-Lee lifted on her toes and lightly brushed her lips across his. "Sounds like a fair compromise. Let's go. I only have to run one race."

"Two." Holt's arm snuck around her waist and drew her close. "You don't think you're going to get away with not racing me?"

She splayed her fingers across his broad chest and laughed. "You're on."

Less than an hour later Emma-Lee put on a helmet. The whine of motors filled the enormous building as people pushed go-karts to the max along the serpentine tracks. Standing close by, Chad, a mechanic on Rafael O'Bryan's team, did likewise. He tipped his fingers in salute and she nodded in return.

Frowning, Holt stepped in front of her and fastened her chin strap. His fingers lingered, tilting her face to his. She recognized the gesture as a man staking out his territory, but she didn't mind. Instead, a thrill streaked through her.

"What's with the deal with the other guy? Why are you racing him in particular?"

"A bet. If I win, he'll let me know when Rafael O'Bryan is in the building so I can set up the interview."

He lowered his hand and she quickly stepped into the car and sat down. The light was sequencing for the next cars to go.

Holt stood behind the line with hands planted on his hips. "And if you lose?"

She kept her eyes on the light. "I pay for dinner at Maudie's."

"What?"

The light flashed green and Emma-Lee and the other driver surged forward. Go-kart driving wasn't about physical strength; it was all about focus, timing and reflexes. She didn't look at the car keeping pace with hers around the first curve. She concentrated on the handling of the kart and mentally played the track course in her head.

Easing into the start of the curve, speeding up as she shot out, gunning on the straight stretches. The roar of the motor, the strain of the metal as the go-kart hurtled forward. It was all about the track and how fast she could drive. Then the car careened around the last corner and the finish was in sight. She let the car go all out and in the last moment she glanced over and knew victory was hers as she sped across the line ahead of Chad's kart.

After she brought the car to a halt, she clambered out. Looking around she spotted Holt grinning in the cheering crowd and he gave her a thumbs-up.

Holding his helmet, Chad approached with his hand out and they shook hands. "Congratulations, Emma-Lee. The deal is for a week, right?"

"One week. If Rafael is in the building, you're to give me a call, nothing more. I'll take it from there."

Chad rubbed the stubble on his chin. "Yes, ma'am. I don't suppose I can throw in treating you to dinner at Maudie's tonight?"

Emma-Lee handed her helmet to the attendant, her gaze locked with Holt's as he advanced toward her. "Sorry, but I have other plans."

Holt gave her a quick hug and then draped his arm around her shoulders. "Savor your win while you can." He guided her toward the line of waiting people. She said goodbye over her shoulder to Chad before turning her attention back to Holt.

"Hey, what's the hurry? Closing time isn't until ten."

"The quicker I beat you in this race, the sooner we can be at the restaurant where I can stare deep into your eyes and tell you how beautiful you are."

Emma-Lee stubbed her toe, but Holt steadied her before she could pitch forward. Beautiful? He thought she was beautiful?

She tossed her head. "You're just trying to distract me."

His mouth curved. "We don't have a bet yet."

"Bet?"

"Yes, since you all are so into competition, shouldn't we also have a stake?"

"Okay." Think of something safe. "Winner springs for dinner?"

Holt shook his head as they stepped nearer to the front of the line. "Nope, I was thinking something a little more personal for my side of the bet."

She swallowed. "How personal?"

"If I win, I get a walk with you and a kiss in the moonlight."

Her stomach jittered. She knew where such an evening might lead. It would entail another risk of her committing to Holt that could lead later to heartache.

Wait a minute. She was safe. No way was she going to lose to him, because she was on a hot streak.

She laughed. "You're on. Be prepared to ante up for a huge steak, for tonight I am one with the track."

EMMA-LEE'S BEING "one with the track" had abandoned her mid-race with him. Recalling her look of chagrin when he had shot past her on the last lap to the finish line, Holt suppressed a smile as he strolled hand in hand with her along the nearly deserted street in Mooresville.

Having guts and instincts were one thing; he had observed those qualities in her as she had raced the other man. However, knowing mathematically the precise moments to slow and accelerate had given him the ultimate advantage. That, plus his almost desperate determination to win.

Being magnanimous in victory, he had treated her to a superb steak dinner in a restaurant dripping with intimacy, from the wood-paneled walls, to the dim lighting, to the unobtrusive service, as he had secured one of the secluded booths.

Candlelight had wrapped its cozy glow around them as she told him stories about her parents and sisters. Still, no matter how discreet the waiter had been, no matter how hidden the booth had been, the low murmur of voices had been a constant reminder that other diners were present.

Upon exiting the restaurant, he'd drawn her along the sidewalk of Main Street. A nearly full moon rode the wave of stars blanketing the night sky. Emma-Lee lifted her face and drew in a deep breath. "I love the scents of spring."

When she turned her head, her eyes held that feminine gleam of awareness. His mouth dried and suddenly, all the things he'd planned to say scattered. Here he'd plotted to have her to himself and now he couldn't form one damn word with his tongue.

"Uh, do you like living here?" Great. That rated in the top all-time romantic conversational starters with a woman.

Then Emma-Lee shifted closer, curling her free hand around his upper arm. The moonlight highlighted the sweet curve of her face as she nodded.

"Yes, I love it here. This was a mill town up until the 1980s so it still has a Sleepy Hollow type of charm. Yet it's not totally off the beaten track because of its being the magic kingdom of NASCAR."

Holt's lips twitched as he released her hand only to circle his arm around her waist to draw her snug against his side. "Magic kingdom?"

She flashed him a grin. "I'm doing it again, aren't I? Reciting facts?"

Recalling how he had yearned to hear her do that very thing this morning, he pressed a kiss on top of her head, the light herbal scent from her shampoo wrapping around his system, tying him in knots.

"Go on. You have a knack for stories like your sister Tara does." A look of disbelief flashed across her face.

He smiled. "Tell me how of all places this hamlet became the pit road of NASCAR universe when it doesn't even have a race track."

"I know. Weird, huh?" Emma-Lee pointed along the street lined with squat buildings. "There you have an over-a-century-old hardware store still in operation. Across the street—" she swung her arm around to where an enormous neon checkered flag sign blazed "—you have the latest and greatest in racing souvenirs."

Of accord they continued, crossing the railroad tracks that had put the mill town on the map. Not wanting the companionable interlude to end, Holt urged softly, "Go on."

Emma-Lee warmed to her subject. "Initially, people associated with the Charlotte track began buying homes around Lake Norman. Soon owners set up shop. By the 1990s Mooresville had souvenir stores, suppliers and even a museum for the hordes of NASCAR fans following the teams here. So the city's leaders, seeing the commercial wave of the future, gave the town the nickname Race City, U.S.A."

Breaking free, she halted and spun around with her arms spread wide. "Voilà, I give you Mooresville."

Laughing, she twirled again. Her mischievous smile aimed over her shoulder at him unerringly found its target, his heart.

Needing her as he'd never craved another in his life, he stepped close and wrapped his arms around her waist. Sensual awareness replaced the laughter in her eyes as he traced her spine with one hand until he could cup the back of her neck.

So soft, so vulnerable. But he couldn't stop there to savor the texture of her skin, for the heavy fall of her hair brushing the back of his hand beckoned. He threaded his fingers through the silky strands that seemed to have a life of their own, circling around to snare his hand.

He wanted to capture her warmth and openness and make her his. Ruthlessly, he yanked a choke chain on the hunger building in him. She was important to him; this was more than the simple sexual byplay that had characterized his life until now.

Drawing her head back, he took his mouth on a slow, quiet journey over her face. When at last he kissed her, edgy need raced through him.

When she melted against him and touched his face, he became bound to her in that moment. There was no turning back from the fall now. The magic that was Emma-Lee had thoroughly captured him. He tightened his hold and took the plunge.

EMMA-LEE FELT HERSELF sliding into the kiss, into Holt. Too often she had danced close to the passion she'd sensed banked in him and now she was caught in the explosion. His kisses were all-consuming fire. Sensations bombarded her, too rapidly for her body to adjust.

As he deepened the kiss, emotions swept through her. She could only grab on to his arms until this heady storm passed.

When his mouth left hers to nibble at the delicate spot behind her ear, dark pleasure flashed through her overcharged system.

This was the man she'd been waiting for.

With a groan Holt again fused his lips to hers in a moist, deep sumptuous kiss that went on endlessly until all thought turned to ashes in her brain.

Love quivered inside her, ready to be given with an open heart. Did she dare or did she care if Holt didn't reciprocate the sentiment?

All she knew was that only he had the power to quench the need growing deep inside her. When his mouth cruised along her throat her head lolled back to give him better access. When he pressed her closer, she slid her leg up along his, craving the strength of his body.

Swept up in the night's embrace of lovers, she opened her eyes and met his gaze. She knew Holt could see into her soul. A shudder rippled through him before he stilled, lifting his head. Regret had replaced desire in his eyes and he stepped away.

With a small cry of protest, she tried to thread her arms around his neck, but he kept her at arm's length. Confusion warred with humiliation and she dropped her hands. When he reached out to touch her, she jerked her head away.

She wrapped pride around her like a shield and said in a voice dripping with icicles. "It's late. We should be heading back."

"Emma-Lee." Holt's hand shot out, his fingers circling her wrist. "I'm sorry."

She wouldn't let him see how hurt she was. "Don't be. We're adults."

He lifted his other hand and cupped her face. Even that simple contact with her still-heated skin sent a shiver racing through her. How was she going to bear this if he didn't want her?

"Honey, how do you survive it?" he asked.

"Survive what?"

"Wearing your emotions on your sleeve? I've never seen anyone who gives so unstintingly all the time."

She bit her lip. "I crash and burn like anyone else. I just get up again."

His gaze intensified. "You scare me sometimes. I don't know if I can give you what you deserve."

His admission eased the pain deep inside her. She pressed

her cheek against his palm and covered his hand with hers. "Why don't you let me be the judge of that?"

"I don't want to hurt you." He shook his head but lowered his hand. "As you said, it's late and tomorrow's a workday for both of us. Let me get you back home." He twined his fingers with hers and started back toward the restaurant.

Emma-Lee walked silently beside him. Holt didn't realize yet that he needed a connection anchoring him between his solitary existence and the rest of humanity.

But hope burned bright, and tonight when she lay in bed she would hug it close to her. Holt had used his first endearment with her. He had called her "honey."

CHAPTER EIGHT

DARLINGTON WAS NOT going as Holt envisioned as he stood out of harm's way behind the pit crew where he'd been left. But when it came to his relationship with Emma-Lee, no plan ever seemed to work.

Take Wednesday night. Even now the memory of how she had burned with passion in his arms haunted him. He had been more than ready to make her his when he'd realized that Emma-Lee's heart had been wrapped up in her willingness to give herself. She hadn't had to say the words. The emotion had been there for him to see in her eyes.

Talk about a cold shower of pure panic.

Another man may have proceeded with the seduction, but he couldn't. Emma-Lee had been prepared to hand him her heart and he had bungled the gift badly. After several sleepless nights, he still didn't know if he could handle it.

So now he was back to the starting line with her: wanting her, needing her, but not sure how to proceed. On the other hand, the minx hadn't appeared to be worse for the separation. She had greeted him with a smile and had gone about the business of taking care of Double S Racing's track guests.

Brooding, he watched the frenetic yet measured pace of the final preparations before the race. Although he had always preferred working alone, he had to admire the display of teamwork.

He glanced down the row and saw other teams similarly engaged in a choreographed dance of man and machine. In war wagons he saw crew chiefs at their computers. He would have loved a look at the programs, but he was stuck watching from the sidelines.

So far his quest to capture Emma-Lee's attention or time had failed. He understood she was working, and yes, she answered all his questions and then some. He learned all about the driver rite of passage known as the Darlington Stripe. However, he heard the information along with a large group of sponsors and guests. Then he'd been herded with a much smaller group to pit road before Emma-Lee had disappeared from sight.

Wasn't it better this way that he didn't have her solely to himself? He didn't have an answer, either for her or himself as to where this relationship was going. He only knew he had to be near her.

With all the activity at the track, he could take a much-needed step back, observe her and analyze his reactions.

Right, Forrester. If you believe that one, there's a corrupted hard drive with your name on it.

His mouth twisted in a rueful smile. For the past hour his system had kicked up a notch every time he had brushed up against Emma-Lee in the crowded garage. Then there had been those few times when her breath had feathered his face when she had leaned close to explain what a team member was doing over the din.

Now his system was so on edge that he was ready to jump into one of the stock cars and race howling around the track.

Hearing her laughter, he absorbed the hit of anticipation as he turned toward the sound. Through the milling crowd, she emerged pushing a wheelchair with a young boy in it. A man and a woman who appeared to be the parents walked on either side of the chair. When the man pointed at one of the cars, the boy's face lit up with an expression of wonderment and he let out a "wooting" sound.

Emma-Lee wheeled her charge right up to the No. 502 car. Holt narrowed his eyes. What was that sticking from the back of the waistband of her jeans?

Standing next to the car, the driver Eli Ward broke off an interview with one of the ubiquitous reporters and shook hands first with the boy and then the dazed-looking parents. Kneeling beside the chair, the driver spoke with the boy for several minutes.

Holt didn't know who had the bigger grin during the conversation, the kid or Emma-Lee. Then she reached behind and whipped out a green baseball cap. She reached into her front pocket and held out a marker pen. Eli took it and with a flourish autographed the cap. Handing the pen to Emma-Lee, the driver ruffled the boy's hair before plopping the hat on top of his head.

Even from his position Holt could see the hero adulation in the kid's eyes. That would be an adrenaline rush, he conceded. He'd always had to find his own satisfaction when data came together and a computer program worked.

The crowd roared as the drivers began the parade around the track. With a start, Holt realized that Emma-Lee was on the move again with the wheelchair, heading straight toward him. He rocked back on his heels and waited.

"Holt, I'd like to introduce you to Phillip Whitney and his parents, Jason and Michele."

He found himself shaking hands with the parents and then the boy. "Nice to meet you. Big NASCAR fans?"

"Yes, sir." Phillip beamed. "I think Eli Ward is the greatest driver ever."

Michele tipped the bill of his cap. "I can't thank Emma-Lee enough for setting this up."

"You're welcome."

Phillip studied Holt. "Do you work for Double S Racing?"

"No, I design computer programs."

The boy's eyes widened. "Games?"

"Well." *Here goes nothing. Time to emerge from behind the monitor.* "I have my first game coming out next month. It's called 'The Mathematician's Secret Chamber.'"

Phillip's mouth fell open. "No fooling? Everyone at school is talking about it. You go through levels searching for a secret wizard?"

So much for keeping quiet about the game. He of all people appreciated the information highway that was the Internet and how rumors spread like wildfire.

Holt grinned. "That's right, with plenty of bad guys trying to stop you at every turn."

Catching the parents and Emma-Lee's puzzled expressions, he explained, "The game takes the player on a search for a famous math wizard who holds an ancient secret and along the way famous mathematicians pop up with clues and the player has to solve a formula."

Understanding lit Emma-Lee's eyes. "You took your father's profession and made a game out of it."

The first game box was already wrapped and ready to mail to Sam.

He hitched a shoulder. "I thought it was a way to get kids to learn about math." He looked at Phillip. "After all, you need to be able to calculate to figure out the rate of fuel consumption, right?"

"Right. I can't wait for the game to come out."

"Tell you what." Holt pursed his lips as if he was coming to a weighty decision. "I need someone to test-drive the game. If you give me your address, I'll send it to you, and you can let me know how it goes."

Phillip swallowed but responded in a nonchalant manner.

"I'd be happy to help out, sir." He rattled off his address, which Holt jotted down.

Emma-Lee's eyes were misty, but she gave them a firm command. "The race is about to start, so we need to clear the area."

After the parents thanked Holt, they moved away with Phillip. They had barely gone ten feet when the boy yelled out, "This is so cool. I'm going to be the first to play the game!"

The same emotion he had experienced at the BASE jump welled up in Holt. Pride, yes, but also the satisfaction of doing something good for another.

The crowd quieted as the parade ended and the drivers rejoined their crews and families. As they walked away, Emma-Lee slipped her arm through his and tilted her head. "You realize you are now a hero in Phillip's book."

Holt realized the punch of gratification must be what drivers such as Eli Ward experienced every time they met a fan. However, the admiration he saw in Emma-Lee's eyes gave him the ultimate rush of pleasure.

He kept his voice casual. "I take it you're still helping the charity coordinator at Double S?"

"Yes, she had a baby boy on Wednesday, so Gil is letting me fill in until she returns. Phillip became paralyzed as a result of a diving accident. His parents wrote that he was a major fan of Eli Ward and would it be possible to get an autographed poster. When I saw that they lived near Darlington—"

"You arranged instead for Phillip to meet Eli in person."

"Yes."

Suddenly, all activity halted as the teams lined up, their caps over their hearts.

Then a female country artist began to belt out the national anthem. Emma-Lee pointed at the sky and he looked up. Against a cloudless canvas, a red, white and blue parachute soared toward the earth, the jumper carrying the American flag. As the last notes of the song faded, the parachutist landed with pinpoint precision.

One glance at Emma-Lee's rapt expression and he knew that she yearned to make that leap. He also realized he would move mountains and bridges to make that happen for her if only…

Stop right there, Forrester. You're stumbling along a path to the future. How about learning first how to commit to a person?

Right.

She tugged his arm. "Come on. I'm to take you up to where the sponsors are sitting."

He shook his head. "I'd rather sit in the stands with the regular fans today." Maybe the smell of rubber would keep her scent from tying his stomach into knots.

She chewed her lower lip, sending his already revved system into overdrive. "Let's get out of the pit area. I'll see what I can do."

She left him standing outside the secured space. The drivers sat in their brightly painted cars, talking last-minute strategy with their crew chiefs. Gil Sizemore walked along the line, pausing to speak with his teams.

"Holt, what are you doing here with Double S Racing?"

He stiffened and turned.

Red-faced, Stan Preston mopped his brow with a monogrammed handkerchief. Despite it being a warm May day in South Carolina, Stan wore a business suit.

"Got an important date, Stan?"

The insurance magnate stepped closer. "As a matter of fact, I do. Meeting with some NASCAR representatives after the race. Plans are moving forward with my owning a race team by 2012."

Stan glanced around and spoke in yet a lower tone. "Things

might go better today if I can say I have an important sponsor already lined up. Do I have your commitment?"

A month ago, Holt knew what his automatic answer would have been. After all, a NASCAR tie would mean good business for his new game. The fan brand loyalty was amazing.

But the circumstances had changed when Emma-Lee had jumped into his life. His mouth curved recalling the moment she had straddled him in the New River Gorge.

The mantra "business is business" may have served him well in the past, but he had just learned that sometimes people needed to come first. His sponsoring another team would hurt Emma-Lee. Holt thrust his hands into his jeans pockets, considering the implications of his urgent need not to hurt her feelings and to protect her.

"I'm sorry, Stan, but I can't sponsor your team."

Preston's face twisted with anger. "Why? Did Gil Sizemore promise you a bigger deal? I can match anything he gave. Let me tell you, I'm going to pay top dollar for the best drivers. I may be able to hire one or two of his better drivers away from the team."

"Stan, not that Gil Sizemore has anything to do with my decision, but somehow I don't think you're going to make a dent in any operation here."

Preston almost went apoplectic. "I may not be from the blue-blooded families of racing, but I have as much capital as anyone here."

"I know you do, Stan." Holt gestured at pit road. "However, I don't think you have the passion and commitment to stay the course like Gil Sizemore and the other team owners show day after day, win or lose. I think racing is as much a plaything as that pro-baseball team you owned for one year. Once you got rid of all the high-priced players, the team started losing. You got bored, sold the team and moved on."

He shrugged. "You can't do that with a car-racing team. Too many people's livelihoods are wrapped up in a team."

He saw Emma-Lee skirt a group of men and head toward him. Time to come clean about his relationship with Preston— but later, when they could be alone. Then he would also tell the Sizemores, whose hospitality he'd been imposing upon.

"My best advice is to think long and hard before you go any further, Stan." Not waiting for a reply, he turned and walked over to Emma-Lee.

She glanced with curiosity at Preston. "A friend of yours?"

"A former business acquaintance," he said as he took her arm, hurrying her out of the way of a golf cart being driven by a security guard.

"Oh." She gazed over her shoulder as he continued walking her toward the stands. "He looks angry."

"He just lost a wager."

When she had shown him to his seat and started to leave, he said, "Stay. Please stay, Emma-Lee. I want to experience the race through your eyes."

She hesitated for only a fraction of a second before she grinned. "I guess I can be on call here as well as anywhere else." She slipped into the seat next to him. Together they stood and cheered as the green flag waved the start of the race. They fought over popcorn, ate ice cream and drank cold sodas.

He slipped his arm around her shoulders as they watched Rafael O'Bryan's No. 408 car scrape the wall, earning him a stripe. Then they stood, yelling together, as Linc Shepherd beat out Rafael in a neck-and-neck sprint across the finish line for a one-two punch for Double S Racing.

When Emma-Lee threw her arms around his neck and kissed him, her joy fizzing like champagne in his system, he took the final plunge, but instead of the dark emotionless abyss inside him he found only light. He didn't know whether he would crash and burn, but take the risk he must to be with this woman.

So he waited while the Double S teams basked in the glory of the victory and until she finished overseeing the tear-down operation.

He watched the day fade into night. By the time she walked from the garage area, intense longing clawed his insides.

When she saw him, looked up at him with those fathomless eyes, he could only hold out his hand.

"Please. Spend the night with me. I need to see the sunrise with you."

Only when she nodded, a smile lighting her face, did hope unfurl deep inside him that maybe, just maybe, he could have a woman's love and not lose her.

TUESDAY MORNING and Emma-Lee hummed as she hurried along the hallway leading to the public entry of Double S Racing. Colorful photographs of drivers, cars and teams, both past and present, covered the walls. As she entered the lobby, Connie, the receptionist, glanced over and grinned.

"Hey, Emma-Lee. Looks like the win at Darlington really brought out the fans today."

Through the glass doors Emma-Lee could see a crowd already milling around and it wasn't ten o'clock yet. Looked like it was going to be a busy day. She couldn't wait.

"Connie, I'm filling in for Peyton this morning. She had to take her daughter to the orthodontist so she's running late."

Connie shook her head. "You gave up the peace and quiet of the executive suite for hordes of screaming kids and cranky adults?"

Emma-Lee leaned against the corner of the desk. "It's only for an hour. Gil's knee-deep in post-race meetings with the teams, so he won't need me until this afternoon. It's a chance for me to learn how the tourist part of the business runs."

Connie chuckled. "Uh-oh. I can't wait to hear what cost-cutting ideas you're going to come up with."

"What do you mean?"

"My husband and I ate at Maudie's last week and Wade Jenkins was going on about how you thought he could save money on paint." Wade handled the detailing of the race cars.

"I only made a suggestion that maybe there was one of those two-in-one paints so he cut out using the base coat."

"And Wade really appreciated the thought." Connie rose and circled the desk. "Time to open the doors."

Emma-Lee adjusted her identification tag. It was show-time.

For a person who loved facts, taking tour groups around the public-access areas of Double S Racing headquarters for an hour was heaven. Imagine having people at your mercy like this all day long. Her mouth curved as she kept a watchful eye on the group as they viewed the work being done on the cars.

However, she now knew what she wanted to do with her life.

Funny how the events of the past few weeks had brought clarity to her choice of careers.

She swiped her suddenly damp palms over her pants. As soon as she was relieved from tour duty, she planned to march right into Gil's office and discuss it with him. Sure, it may be a while before the position actually came open. And if it didn't…

She'd jump that bridge when she came to it.

"Emma-Lee."

She turned and smiled at the woman behind her. "Hi, Peyton. How did the orthodontist appointment go?"

Peyton, a mother of two young girls, winced. "Expensive. Denise needs braces."

"Yikes. Good thing we have good health insurance here."

"You better believe it." Peyton leaned closer. "Emma-Lee, Gil needs to see you immediately, so I'll take over this group. Thanks for filling in."

"No problem." Emma-Lee said goodbye and then made her way to the executive suite. Gil's door was closed, so she gave a quick rap.

"Come in."

Entering, she saw Marley Sizemore sitting in one of the two client chairs. Gil rose and gestured toward the empty chair.

"Emma-Lee. Please have a seat."

He didn't offer his easy smile and Marley looked somber. In fact, tension in the room was so palpable that she could have cut it with a blowtorch.

Uh-oh. She sat down. "Is something wrong?"

Gil clasped his hands on top of the desk. "Possibly. What do you know about Stan Preston?"

She was good with names but drew a blank on this one. "I don't think I know him. Why?"

"Are you sure? Holt Forrester was spotted talking with Stan Preston this weekend at Darlington."

She recalled the angry man who had been with Holt.

"Oh. Holt did run into a former business acquaintance, but I wasn't introduced to him."

She sensed the tension easing from both Sizemores. "I'm sorry, but who is this Stan Preston?"

Gil answered. "He's the owner of a number of insurance agencies. Has made a fortune over the years. He's meeting with NASCAR officials about starting a new racing team. On Saturday he gave Holt's name as one of his sponsors."

Confusion swirled inside her. She looked from Gil to Marley and then back to Gil. "I don't understand…"

Regret flickered in Gil's eyes. "I think Holt's been using his connection with you to get an inside track on racing."

Emma-Lee sat forward. "Holt wouldn't spy for this other man, if that's what you are implying!"

"I'm not, Emma-Lee." Gil shook his head. "I checked him out the first time he came to the tracks. He has a solid reputation in the business world. He's sharp, with good instincts when it comes to trends in computers and software. However, he's acted as a software consultant for Preston in the past."

Her stomach twisted. "But Holt contacted us about donating racing memorabilia for the breast cancer fundraiser. I'm the one who invited him to the Richmond race."

"Being the astute businessman he is, Holt probably saw the invite as a golden opportunity to get an insider's view before committing to a sponsorship."

Emma-Lee wanted the floor to open and swallow her up. The threat of tears scalded her eyes, but she straightened her shoulders and thrust her chin forward. "You mean he's been using me."

Marley leaned forward and lightly touched her arm. "If it helps, Gil and I both liked him and were using the opportunity to court him for a sponsorship."

Emma-Lee gave them her brightest smile. "In other words, all's fair when it comes to doing business."

"Of course not." Marley sounded aghast. "But I wanted to let you know we, too, were taken in by him."

"Oh." Emma-Lee studied her tightly linked fingers. "Sorry."

"We just wanted to let you know about the situation," Gil said gently.

"Thank you."

"However, given the circumstances, Double S will not be giving him passes anymore."

"Trust me. That's not going to be a problem." She rose. "Is there anything else?"

Gil wore a troubled expression, but he leaned back in his chair. "I had a message that you wanted to speak with me today if I had time."

The charity coordinator position. She might as well kiss that goodbye for a while. She had just been played for a sucker. Why would the Sizemores entrust her with such an important position now?

"Nothing urgent." Her voice was brittle. "The matter can wait."

"Is the interview set up with Rafael yet?"

"No, I haven't been able to corner him yet."

Gil's mouth curved. "He's wily."

"But I promise you, the interview will be a done deal by the NASCAR Sprint All-Star Race."

She spun around and left the office. It was all she could do not to run down the hall. Since there was no privacy at her desk, she went to the charity coordinator's vacant office and closed the door.

She unclipped her cell phone and with trembling fingers hit the speed-dial number for Holt.

"Emma-Lee." Even though she knew him for what he was, his saying her name still had the power to send shivers racing along her spine. What did that make her?

A fool in love. One who had given her body and soul to a man who had used her.

She blinked back the tears and steeled herself.

"Answer one question, Holt."

There was a pause before Holt asked cautiously, "What's wrong, honey?"

"Were you ever going to tell me about Stan Preston?"

The acute silence shattered whatever remained of her aching heart.

"I see."

"No, I planned to tell you everything at Darlington, but then…"

"You got an extra dividend by taking me to bed as you were sealing the sponsorship deal with him."

"That's not how it was, Emma-Lee. I'll fly there tonight and we can have dinner. I'll explain everything."

"Don't bother, Holt. I trusted you, I trusted you with…"

She paused. She had almost said "her heart." Have some pride, Dalton. This is the original Tin Man. He wouldn't know a heart if it whacked him on his hard head.

She inhaled a deep breath. "Holt, let's get real. Our relationship never stood a chance. You're so much more connected to that black-and-white world of microbits than you'll ever be with people. I'm sorry, but I put people first."

She hit the disconnect button and then sank down. Wrapping her arms around her middle, she let the tears come.

CHAPTER NINE

HOLT STOOD in the classroom doorway, watching the older version of himself scrawling an equation across the chalkboard. Sam Forrester's shoulders may have been thinner and more stooped than he recalled, but his father's face still bore its trademark stamp of intelligence and intense focus.

Holt slipped his hands into the pockets of his jacket. It had been a long day and the worst was yet to come. After Emma-Lee's call, he had tried to throw himself back into the launch of the computer game. However, as he had stared into his laptop screen, he had realized the bubble of isolation in which he lived had finally burst. He could have a future if it included Emma-Lee.

So he had started with the easiest break to mend: the present. He had flown to Mooresville and met with the Sizemores. They had accepted his apology with that bone-deep Southern class of theirs. However, they had welcomed with even greater enthusiasm his proposal to develop improved software for their racing teams.

Now to confront his past.

"Hello, Dad."

The older man froze and then slowly turned. "Holt, I wasn't expecting you."

Holt strolled down the stairs past the long rows of benches. Many a night in his youth he had sat here working on his homework as Sam Forrester had set up the complex formulas for his next day's classes. Then they would go to the cafeteria for dinner before heading home, where Sam would immediately disappear into his study to work on his book.

A lonely man, a lonely boy. He didn't want to end up like his father.

Holt halted beside the desk and placed the game disk on top. "How are you doing, Dad?"

Sam laid down the chalk and wiped his hands on a handkerchief. "I'm fine. What's this?"

"My first computer game. It's called 'The Mathematician's Secret Chamber.'"

Sam reached out a trembling hand and touched the brightly colored jacket. "A game about math?"

Dismayed by the signs of his father's aging, Holt slid his hands into his pockets so he wouldn't fist them. "Yes. I've named the secret wizard Samuel, after you."

That last-minute change had cost a small fortune, but as his father's face lit up, he realized it had been worth every penny.

"Thank you, Holt. That means a lot to me." Sam tapped the game again. "You'll reach more people than I ever did with my book."

He removed his hands and spread them. "Don't say that, Dad. This is a game. Your book..." Holt recalled the pride he had experienced when he had read it. "Your book was an illumination on a new theory."

"You read it?"

"Yes, I did." He continued in a rush, "I'm sorry. After Mom's death, I blamed you for not being there for me. I realize now how hard it must have been for you to lose her."

Sam shot him a startled look as he lowered himself into the old chair behind the desk. "Amanda was the emotional connector among us all and when she died, I was so lost."

He shook his head. "I was the adult, son, and I should have figured out how to be a better father to you. I just didn't have

Amanda's people skills. However, I've always been proud of you and the man you've become."

Holt swallowed back the lump the size of a hard drive in his throat. "You wouldn't be so proud of me at the moment. I'm in trouble."

He folded his arms across his chest. "There's a woman."

Unbelievably, Sam's lips curved into a smile and he made a raspy sound that sounded suspiciously like a chuckle. "There always is when a man is troubled."

Stunned, Holt almost fell over. "The thing is, she's a real people person. I've never met anyone able to connect like she does."

"And you're wondering what she sees in a loner like you?"

"Yes. No." He raised a hand and ran his fingers through his hair. "I don't know."

Sam's expression grew distant as he stared out at the classroom. "I experienced the same panic when I met your mother. How could anyone with so much life possibly be interested in someone like me? It was like being a moth drawn to a flame."

His father had never talked about the early days with his mother. Intrigued, Holt asked, "How did you meet?"

Sam's eyes warmed. "At college. I was sitting between classes reading under a tree when the most gorgeous girl in the world literally fell in my lap. She had been chasing a Frisbee and wasn't watching where she was running."

Holt stilled. He didn't believe in déjà vu, but a wave of inevitability swept through him.

Lost in his memories, Sam continued, "She laughed as she apologized. When Amanda smiled, it was as if this beam of sun lightened everything inside me. I was hooked."

He clasped his hands together and glanced up at Holt. "I never regretted marrying her. When she fell ill and left us, I was devastated. But if I had to go back to that moment on the campus green, I would stick out my foot to trip her all over again."

Dazed, Holt shook his head. "Dad, did I hear you right? Mom didn't fall?"

Sam flashed an unrepentant grin that Holt hadn't seen since before his mother had gotten ill. "Nope. Amanda was the prettiest girl on campus and when I saw her running toward me I knew I had to seize the moment to make her notice me.

"So." He leaned forward. "What mess have you gotten yourself in and what are you going to do to land your woman?"

FROM THE REAR BOOTH of Maudie's Down Home Diner where she had taken refuge, Emma-Lee stared out at car headlights gleaming on the rain-slick street. The late-spring storm suited her dismal mood.

"Emma-Lee, is there something wrong with the meat loaf?"

Emma-Lee blinked. Looking anxious, the waitress, Mellie Donovan, stood beside her, holding a cleaning rag. Mellie gestured toward the kitchen. "We're getting ready to close for the night, but I'm sure Sheila won't mind if I asked the cook to whip you up something else."

Despite her mood, Emma-Lee managed to smile. "What? And delay the start of the Tuesday Tarts session? She would have my hide."

Sheila Trueblood not only ran Maudie's Down Home Diner with a firm and efficient hand, she also hosted the weekly gathering of women known as the Tuesday Tarts in the back room of the restaurant. While those who attended might vary from week to week, the purpose was always the same as they sat around the table and drank whatever wine someone brought in: to gossip, laugh and in general give moral support.

Emma-Lee had almost skipped this week's Tuesday Tarts

session. She had no experience hiding a broken heart, but in the end her friend—and hairdresser—Daisy Brookshire had convinced her to come. There had been recent sightings of Rafael O'Bryan at the restaurant, and she was on a desperate mission to prove herself once and for all to the Sizemores. She couldn't screw this up.

She picked up the plate of food she had only picked at and handed it to Mellie. "The meat loaf was delicious as always. It turned out that I didn't have the appetite I thought I would."

The waitress nodded. "I'll box it for you."

Two tables over several men from PDQ Racing rose. As the others headed toward the entrance, driver Bart Branch cut over to the rear booth where Emma-Lee sat. Although he gave her a friendly nod, his gaze never left the waitress's face.

"Mellie, we're leaving now. See you next week."

The young woman's eyes sparkled. "Goodnight, Bart."

He brushed close to her as he strolled away.

Hmm, Emma-Lee thought. *Looks like Bart has a crush on Mellie. Interesting.*

She cleared her throat. "Mellie?"

The waitress stopped watching the driver. A faint blush crept across her cheeks. "I'm sorry, Emma-Lee. You said something?"

Oh, yeah. A two-way crush definitely in the making. She perked up.

"How's Lily? I haven't seen her."

Mellie's expression brightened at the mention of her daughter. "She's fine, playing upstairs with Louise." Louise Jordan was the cook Al's wife, who had taken to watching Lily while Mellie worked.

The door opened and several women walked in. Emma-Lee grinned when she saw Rue Larrabee saunter toward the back of the restaurant. An impossible shade of red was the hair color *du jour* for the flamboyant owner of the Cut 'N' Chat

Beauty Salon. Behind her waddled the pregnant Daisy Brook-shire, one of Rue's stylists. Rounding out the group was Susie, driver Ben Edmonds's wife.

"Looks like the meeting is about to begin. I'll bring your food right back."

"You're not joining us?"

"No. The diner's been busy today. I haven't had much time to be with Lily all day. However, I'll bring Lily down to say hi since she asked earlier if she was going to see you."

"Here." Emma-Lee rummaged in her purse for her wallet and removed money. "Go ahead and ring me up. Mustn't keep the Tarts waiting."

She noticed Gil Sizemore had sauntered up to the cash register where Sheila stood ringing up orders. As he paid, he leaned toward her. Whatever he said had the restaurant owner laughing. Why hadn't Emma-Lee ever noticed before that her boss might have a thing for Sheila?

Emma-Lee rubbed a palm over the ache in her chest. Did having a broken heart mean she was more attuned to the possibility of love for others?

Gil started for the door but changed course and came toward her. Emma-Lee's immediate thought was to slide down the booth, but she straightened her shoulders and smiled. "Good evening, Gil."

"Emma-Lee." He hooked his thumbs in his pockets. "I saw your application for the charity coordinator's job. Why don't you come see me first thing in the morning and we'll discuss it?"

She swallowed and struggled to keep her voice even. "I'd be happy to, Gil."

"Good night." He gave her a wink, turned and strolled out of the restaurant.

Oh, boy. Excitement bubbled inside her. Her shot at a career she wanted was going to happen after all.

She glanced around and realized the crowd had thinned considerably. On the opposite side a dark-complected man rose with two others. Emma-Lee's pulse quickened.

The elusive Rafael O'Bryan at long last.

She leaped to her feet and raced past the line of booths and the photographs of NASCAR's legendary drivers past and present adorning the walls. Reaching the front, she planted herself square in the driver's path.

He looked irritated but muttered an "excuse me" as he tried to circle around her.

"Oh, no, you don't, Rafael." She blocked him as she fisted her hands on her hips.

"I have been trying to speak with you for the past two weeks. You won't return my calls or respond to my messages."

"I'm busy, Emma-Lee. Catch me when the season is over."

Time to toss out the big gun's name. "Gil Sizemore, remember him? He's your boss. Well, he's asked me to set up an interview with *Sports Scene* magazine. Do you want me to report to him that one of his drivers is too busy to do interviews? That he's too busy for his fans?"

A dull red flush crept up the driver's neck. He jammed his hands into his jacket pockets. "Fine. Set it up. I'll be there. Now may I leave?"

Victory sure tasted sweet. Chivalrously, Emma-Lee stepped aside and made a sweeping gesture. Rafael stormed past her followed by his two companions, who were grinning ear to ear.

The door swung closed. Cheers broke out. Swinging around, she first bowed to the Tarts standing in a circle behind her and then pumped her fist.

"Way to go, Emma-Lee." Sheila Trueblood folded her arms across her chest. "Now let's head back and you can tell us all why earlier you looked like a truck ran over you."

A draft of rain-chilled air swept in as the door opened. Sheila gave the new visitor a polite smile. "Someone will be right with you."

The hairs lifted on the nape of Emma-Lee's neck and an acute awareness prickled. Even before she turned, she knew who stood behind her.

Ridiculous.

She turned and absorbed the one-two punch of love and hurt. Holt wore his battered bomber jacket over a forest-green shirt. The well-worn jeans molded his toned body. Droplets of rain glistened in his wind-mussed sandy hair. Under one arm he carried two packages.

But tonight his set jaw and the intense gaze of his hazel eyes gave him a predatory look, and *she* was his target.

One of the women behind her, most likely Rue, muttered, "Hubba hubba."

She cleared her throat and, aware of the curious stares and listening ears, said in a low tone, "Holt, why are you here?"

He reached out and toyed with the ends of her hair. "You haven't returned any of my messages."

"I did. I told you it was over." Unable to hear his voice, afraid she would cave and listen to his explanations, she had texted him once.

"Oh, yes, I recall that very civilized text message." His mouth thinning, he lowered his head. "I never would have thought you such a coward, Emma-Lee."

He was one furious male, she realized with a start. What right did he have to be angry? He was the one who had used her. She wrapped her arms around her middle. "I don't want to see you anymore, Holt. You lied to me."

"I did not—" He broke off on a muffled oath and cast a meaningful glance at the other women. "Can we go somewhere to discuss this?"

Although scenes weren't particularly her forte, people

weren't his. So long as she remained here she was safe from her foolish heart that even now wanted him.

She tilted her chin. "Whatever you have to say will have to wait. The Tuesday Tarts are in session."

"Hear, hear."

"You go, girl."

Emboldened, she swept out an arm in dramatic fashion. "You'll have to leave now."

Maybe she did have a little of her sister Mallory's acting ability after all.

"You want to air this in front of your friends, then fine." Holt dropped the plastic-wrapped packages on the nearest table with a resounding thud.

Not the result Emma-Lee had expected. *Steady, girl.* She drew in a deep breath and smelled the intoxicating scent of rain, leather and male. Not helping the nerves. She exhaled.

He gave the Tarts a nod. "Excuse me, ladies." Then he looked at her with a naked expression that jolted her. It was as if all barriers he'd erected against the world had been stripped away and there was only the two of them.

"You think I used you."

"Let me think." Since her natural impulse was to touch, to connect, she clasped her hands behind her. "All the while I was letting you view Double S's operations, you were planning to sponsor your friend's new racing team. Of course you were using me."

Exasperation flashed across his face. "You parachuted into my lap, remember? You were the one who invited me to the Richmond race."

Emma-Lee bit her lip to keep it from trembling. "You should have said something then."

"I'd only met you. I was attracted to you. I saw your offer as a way of killing two birds with one stone. Get a closer look at stock car racing before investing in it while keeping company with a beautiful, charming woman."

She didn't think her heart could hurt anymore. "It was just business to you." She turned her head so he couldn't see her pain.

He simply put a hand under her chin, lifted it until their eyes met. "Learning about racing, yes. Becoming involved with you, no."

Holt looked so intent, so sincere that everything around her faded.

"The moment I realized that I couldn't separate the two anymore and you could be hurt, I told Preston that I couldn't be a sponsor."

Everything inside her stilled. "When?"

"At Darlington. That's the conversation you interrupted. I was telling him then that it wouldn't work. In fact, I told him that he's not suited for the world of NASCAR and he should give up the idea. He doesn't have the dedication and passion for the sport."

"What about the Sizemores? You used them, too."

He rubbed his thumb along her jawline. "I met with them and apologized. We've come to an understanding. I've offered to redesign some of their software programs.

"Honey." He dropped his hand only to wrap an arm around her waist and slowly drag her against his body to the hoots of the Tarts. Desperate to maintain some space between them, she splayed her hands against his chest and shoved, but it was like trying to move a mountain.

"Not only did I make peace with the Sizemores, I made peace with my father."

"What?"

He nodded at the table covered with packages. "One of those is the game cartridge for your friend Phillip. The other is an autographed copy of Dad's book for you."

"You saw your father?" She could scarcely breath. Had they finally bridged the gap left in their lives by Amanda Forrester's death? Hope fluttered to life once more inside her.

"We talked about Mom—cleared the air." Holt hitched a shoulder. "I knew I had to make peace with the past in order to move into the future."

"Emma-Lee." He stroked a strand of hair away from her face. "I'm sorry."

"Holt, I'm glad that you apologized to the Sizemores and reconnected with your dad, but that won't change things between us. We're both too wary in our own ways to take a chance on a relationship."

With a smile he shook his head. "I disagree. I think we're both made a turn in our lives. I know I have and it brought me to you." His arm tightened around her.

"Emma-Lee, what do you want to do with your life? Forget about your family or anyone else's expectations, what career will bring you fulfillment?"

The blaze in his eyes consumed her. She swallowed. "Charity coordinator. I want to be Double S's charity coordinator."

He pressed a featherlight kiss on the tip of her nose. "You'll be perfect as the charity coordinator. I can't imagine anyone more born for the role than you."

Holt raised his head only a fraction. His warm breath fanned her face. "Emma-Lee Dalton, you've always been a risk-taker. Does that big heart of yours have enough room to save me from spending the rest of my life in isolated darkness?"

The packages on the table were more than a game and a book. They represented the connections to people he had made and the changes he had made in his life, changes that could mean a place for their relationship. A man who could walk away from a business deal, a man who could reconnect with his father, a man who could fight in front of a crowd—this was a man who she could trust with her heart.

She raised trembling hands and framed his face. "I love you, Holt."

He wrapped his arms around her, hauling her up. "It took nearly losing you for me to figure it out, but I love you, too, Emma-Lee."

As he kissed her, all the pieces of her life coalesced into stunning clarity. Dimly, she heard the shouts of the Tarts. Then there was only Holt.

EXCITEMENT VIBRATED in the air at the speedway. Last-minute preparations continued at breakneck speed as race time drew near. Holt watched the teams line up and place their caps over their hearts while a local military guard played the national anthem. As the announcer told the crowd to look up, a plane flew overhead and several forms jumped out.

At first there were only bright splashes of color against the deep translucent blue of the twilight sky. Then as the parachutist fell closer to the ground, he made out the instructor he'd contracted strapped to another carrying the snapping American flag. Pride swelled in Holt's chest as chutes blossomed and the stand erupted into cheers.

Beside him Jeffrey Colton cleared his throat. Holt could feel a knot in his throat forming as he could now see the beaming grin on Sandy Colton's face as the instructor maneuvered the pair toward the circle that had been painted on the infield. Emma-Lee landed beside them.

Photographers and reporters raced forward as Emma-Lee made a bull's-eye landing. Several men grabbed the chutes while others helped the divers from the harnesses. In the glow of the spotlights and to the roar of the crowd, Sandy, wearing a red, white and blue scarf, waved the flag in triumph. The cheers grew louder as Jeff raced forward to kiss his wife.

He walked up to Emma-Lee and, laughing with the sheer joy of life that was unique to her, she threw her arms around his neck.

"Oh, Holt, I can't thank you enough for setting this all up! For the few moments we were free-falling, Sandy yelled that she was flying."

She glanced over her shoulder at the other couple still locked arm in arm as they faced reporters. "This meant the world to her and me."

Holt tightened his hold, drawing her closer. "And you brought me back into the world, Emma-Lee Dalton. Business may be business, but in this life, my true bottom line is love."

He lowered his head and kissed her, sealing the deal.

* * * * *

Cornered

Maggie Price

To Al and Merline Lovelace—true blue friends
and the best travel companions in the entire world.

CHAPTER ONE

RAFAEL O'BRYAN LEANED forward in the chair across from his boss's expansive mahogany desk. "My sponsor wants me to do what?"

"Get with the program," Gil Sizemore replied.

"Meaning?"

"Acer Carpenter, the CEO of National Steel Buildings, called me last night. He and certain board members are concerned they're not getting a substantial return on the investment they've made in you and your team. One concern is your uneven race finishes so far this year."

Rafael set his jaw. He couldn't exactly object. He'd won at Daytona in February. It was now June, and his finishes in the succeeding NASCAR Sprint Cup Series races had been inconsistent. His team was new this year, still working to get its rhythm. Even so, that was no excuse. NSB had sponsored the team expecting impressive performances. *He* was the one who climbed into the driver's seat on race days. Ultimately his actions mattered most.

"You said Carpenter and the NSB board have concerns. Plural. What are the others?"

"There's just one more, but it's major." As he spoke, Gil raked his fingers through his dark hair. "You don't exactly welcome media attention."

Here we go, Rafael thought. He'd heard much the same comment from sponsors of other teams he'd driven for. He'd had no choice but to handle those situations to suit his own needs. He would deal with this one the same way. "I never turn down requests for pre- or post-race interviews."

"Those interviews always focus on that day's race and your driving."

"Which is what my fans want to hear about."

"Not according to your sponsor. NSB believes your fans want to know more than just what strategy you used on the track during a specific race. They want to learn about what you do in your off time. Get a look into your home life. Find out about the women you date. Bottom line, they want to know what makes Rafael O'Bryan tick."

"That's why I write a monthly e-mail newsletter for my fans." It contained only the information about himself that he wanted known. Some of it was true. Same thing went for the personal data listed in his official bio.

"I've seen the newsletter." Gil settled back in his dark leather chair. Dressed in a team polo shirt and khaki pants, the owner of Double S Racing in no way resembled a scion of Charleston blue bloods. But that was exactly what he was.

Rafael gave thanks daily that Gil was the Sizemore family's maverick whose keen interest in NASCAR had prompted him to relocate to North Carolina in order to establish Double S Racing. Other drivers and teams also operated under the Double S banner, but Gil freely admitted he'd put a team together for Rafael specifically to give him a shot at the NASCAR Sprint Cup Series championship that had so far eluded him.

For that reason, Rafael felt a huge sense of loyalty toward his boss. But it tugged and tangled against the commitment he'd made to others years ago when he left his native Brazil.

"Maybe NSB's CEO and board members haven't seen my fan newsletter. I'll make sure they're on the distribution list."

"Won't hurt," Gil said. "But that's not going to solve your problem. You participate in a sport that demands its athletes step into the spotlight. NASCAR fans are loyal, they buy the products their favorite drivers represent. NSB hasn't seen the big bump in sales they anticipated after they took on sponsorship of you and your team. That doesn't make them happy."

Rafael frowned. "During negotiations, you told them I wouldn't do televised commercial spots to hawk their products. Acer Carpenter agreed to the stipulation."

"That hasn't changed."

"All right." Rafael eased out a breath. He knew there was no way a NASCAR Sprint Cup Series driver could totally avoid the limelight. Knew, too, that on any given race day his image might be televised worldwide. But so were pictures of numerous other drivers, and for that reason, he felt safe enough that he blended into the crowd.

What he didn't want was for his face to show up day after day in a commercial that might be broadcast on Brazilian TV. Granted, his appearance had changed greatly over the years. The chance was minute that he might be identified by the man whose presence he'd spent very little time in when he was a scruffy-looking teenager. Still, others were in harm's way and it was a chance Rafael wasn't willing to take.

"What exactly does NSB want me to do?"

"Let a reporter follow you around for the majority of the month of June."

"A month?"

Gil nodded. "A sort of 'a month in the life of a Sprint Cup Series driver.' A profile that will encompass the next three races, and come out soon after the race in New Hampshire."

"Come out in what? A newspaper?"

"No, *Sports Scene* magazine."

Rafael shook his head. *Sports Scene* had international distribution. "I can't agree to that."

"You already did. Emma-Lee hit you up about doing an interview with the magazine," Gil countered, referring to his personal assistant. "But when she tried to get you to commit to a firm date, you blew her off. That won't work this time."

Gil paused, then shook his head. "Look, I know you took a lot of ribbing from the team after *People* magazine ran your picture and dubbed you 'the heartthrob of NASCAR.' But that was the season before last when you were a hair away from winning the Sprint Cup Series championship. Water under the bridge. And articles in *Sports Scene* tend to focus on an athlete's abilities, not his or her looks, so history isn't likely to repeat itself."

The *heartthrob* moniker had barely fazed him, Rafael thought. The ribbing he'd taken over it had been a minor annoyance. What *had* bothered him was seeing his photo plastered across an entire page of the magazine, leaving no chance that his image would blend in with pictures of other drivers. He'd held his breath that a copy of the magazine wouldn't wind up in the wrong hands. After two years, he figured he'd dodged that bullet. Now, he apparently had another one to avoid.

"I still don't like the idea of a reporter shadowing me for a month."

Gil leaned forward slowly, his gaze narrowed. "Carpenter and the board love this idea. If you want NSB to remain your sponsor, you're going to have to agree to this. It's midseason. There's no way I could arrange another sponsor for you at this point. So if you want to keep driving for Double S Racing, you'll go along with NSB's wishes. This is nonnegotiable."

Hands fisted, Rafael rose, strode across the second-floor office to the waist-to-ceiling wall of glass that looked down on the garage. As always, the work center was spotless, the floor immaculate. Mechanics and other crew members were preparing the gleaming black No. 499 car for Sunday's race at Pocono. The car would be loaded into the hauler and leave for the track the following day.

Gazing at the NSB decal that stretched across the hood, Rafael couldn't imagine not being able to climb behind the wheel. Driving was more than just a job. It was his passion. Out on a race track, sitting in the driver's seat, was the only place where he could shut down the pretense, shift mentally into race mode and be who he really was.

He needed that sense of freedom. Not to mention his earnings. He wasn't the only person dependent on them. Without a sponsor, he couldn't race. There would be no money coming in to continue the shipments.

"Rafael, NSB has a valid point. If you held back on the race track the way you do where PR is concerned, you and I would have an insurmountable problem."

Rafael turned from the window. Gil had left his chair and was now leaning against the front of the desk, arms crossed over his chest. "I would never hold back on the track. You know that."

"Yes, I do. That's one reason you're driving for my company. You and your team are new to Double S Racing. I understand that everyone is still working to get in stride with each other. If that happens soon, you'll have a good shot at winning this year's championship. But all bets are off if NSB walks away."

"I understand."

"So, cooperate. *Sports Scene* magazine contacted Emma-Lee again. They're sending George Grant to write the profile. He's got an appointment with me this afternoon to get an overview of Double S. Then he'll hook up with you this evening at NSB's employee health fair where you're scheduled to sign autographs. Grant's covered NASCAR for years, so I imagine he's interviewed you before."

Rafael pictured the tall silver-haired reporter. A couple of times Grant had snagged him for short interviews before and after races. "A time or two."

"Then you know from experience he has the reputation as a straight shooter. All you have to do is let George follow you around for a couple of weeks while you tell him about your past and present. You do that, everybody will be happy."

And a few people might wind up dead, Rafael thought.

Gil pushed away from the desk. "What do you say? Do I tell Acer Carpenter that you'll go along with this?"

Rafael glanced across his shoulder at the gleaming black car. Driving wasn't his only skill. He also knew what it took to survive. He had proven that while living on the crime-infested streets of São Paulo where life could come to a sudden, violent end at any time. Only two other people knew about that dark and murky part of his past.

And that Rafael O'Bryan wasn't his given name.

He had legally changed his name when he moved to the States, and he would do whatever else it took to guard his secrets and keep the people he loved safe.

He looked back at his boss. "Relax, Gil. You can count on me to give George Grant the exact information he needs to write the profile."

YOU CAN PULL THIS OFF, Caitlin Dempsey told herself as she wheeled her rental car into a parking spot in front of Double S Racing's headquarters building. *After all, you've written about hundreds of sports figures. This is just one more to add to the list.*

Admittedly most of those athletes had been involved in some sort of scandal. Which was the type of meaty, dig-for-the-truth-no-matter-what-it-took story Caitlin preferred to tackle. But circumstances in the form of a fellow journalist's family medical emergency had sent this assignment her way, so here she was, about to embark on a month-long interview of an athlete whose sport she'd never covered and knew little about.

After turning off the engine, she stared through the windshield at the three-story brick building with windows tinted a smoky gray. Well-maintained beds of flowering shrubs and colorful annuals bordered the front, looking as bright as gems in the noonday sun.

The knot of nerves in her stomach served as a reminder that she had never before walked into an interview without having a solid understanding of the sport in which a celebrity athlete participated. And, dammit, she hated that feeling. Hated knowing that when it came to NASCAR, the only research she'd had time to conduct was a fast read of the information in the bulging file folder George Grant had shoved into her hands early that morning. She'd met George at the hospital where his only daughter had been taken after a car broadsided hers, leaving her seriously injured.

Understandably, the veteran reporter had been in no condition to answer any specific questions about NASCAR. So Caitlin had used the flight time from New York to Charlotte to start boning up on stock car racing. In truth, she felt like an errant college student who'd ditched class all semester, and was now desperately cramming for the final.

To make matters more complicated, not only was she flying blind about all things NASCAR, but about Rafael O'Bryan, too.

Grabbing her leather portfolio off the seat beside her, she slid out of the car, then smoothed a hand over her pencil-slim black skirt. Her high heels clicked sharply along the flower-bordered sidewalk that led to the building's entrance.

She had studied O'Bryan's picture on the flight for so long

that his image was now branded into her brain. Just under six feet tall, he looked hard edged and physical in a way that suggested solid gym time. His olive skin, thick black hair and Viking-blue eyes evidenced the mixed Latino and Irish heritage background mentioned in his official bio. She would definitely make note of those striking looks when she wrote the profile on him.

Striking looks, she thought, and rolled her eyes. *Gorgeous* had been the first thought that popped into her brain the instant she saw his picture. The reporter for *People* magazine who'd dubbed O'Bryan *the heartthrob of NASCAR* had scored a direct hit.

Which was neither here nor there, Caitlin reminded herself as she started up the steps leading to the building's entrance. Sometimes it seemed to her the sports world was overloaded with good-looking males. She had interviewed an uncountable number of them. Rafael O'Bryan might be one of the hottest-looking race car drivers on the circuit, but his looks made no difference. She would sink her teeth into this project by learning all she could about the man's past and present, then sprinkle those facts throughout the profile. After that, she would move on to the next project her editor assigned to her.

She'd resolved a long time ago that moving on was the safest way to live her life. On those rare times when she crossed paths with a man whom she sensed might be a little hard to distance herself from, she forced herself to take a hard look at the scars she'd earned to remind herself how life really worked. That was all it took for her to move on, both physically and emotionally.

She had just reached for one of the building's heavy glass entry doors when it swung outward, jolting her arm. The unexpected blow sent her skittering back, one of her spiked heels catching between a seam in the concrete. She swore aloud as she stumbled awkwardly, hampered by the narrow skirt that ended just above her knees. The only thing that saved her from going down were the hands that latched on to her upper arms.

"Steady."

She looked up into a pair of bright blue eyes, and everything inside her went still. *That face.* It was the one that had seared into her brain during her flight. Yet it was different from what had been captured by the magazine's photographer. In person, there was a toughness about Rafael O'Bryan's face, a hardness that had to do with more than tanned skin tight over bones. It wasn't a kind one, she thought. There was too much living in it, too much knowledge, for kindness. And in the depths of those laser-blue eyes, she saw secrets.

People with secrets posed a distinct challenge for the reporter in her.

"Sorry. Are you okay?"

His mouth held no softness whatsoever, but his voice was smooth and warm like a fine brandy, almost seductive, a little concerned. The rich Portuguese accent made her knees weak.

"Fine," she managed to say. "I'm fine. No harm done."

"Glad to hear it." For a second, maybe two, he stood staring down at her, his hands still gripping her arms. The touch of his flesh against hers was inconsequential. Except for the sudden burst of heat.

Whoa. Her fingers clenched on the handle of her portfolio. Where did *that* come from?

Something flickered in his eyes then was gone, making her wonder if he'd felt it, too. His hands slid down her arms, grazing her fingers as he released her.

She took a step back. He wore a starched white shirt that was open at the collar, the cuffs rolled up on strong, tanned forearms. The shirt was paired with pressed black jeans that molded his powerful legs.

She felt a sudden vulnerability that she hadn't felt in years—and had sworn to never feel again. Straightening her spine, she did a mental shake of her head. She was back on her feet physically. Time to get the inner balance she worked so hard to maintain under control.

"Mr. O'Bryan, I'm Caitlin Dempsey, *Sports Scene* magazine." As she spoke, she pulled a business card out of the side pocket of her portfolio. "I understand we'll be working together on a profile for the next month."

His dark brows rose as he accepted the card. "And I understood I'd be working with George Grant. Are you his assistant?"

"Replacement. I happened to be in our editor's office when George called to say his daughter had been injured in a car wreck. I'd just wrapped up my latest assignment, so I got tagged to replace George." She angled her chin. "My editor said he would have his secretary phone Double S Racing to let your boss know about the change. Sounds like that didn't happen."

"It didn't." Rafael glanced at her card, studied it for a long moment, then those electric-blue eyes remet hers. Good Lord, if there was ever a man who looked like the kind of fantasy a woman didn't want to wake up from, this guy was it.

"Are you as much an expert on NASCAR as your colleague?" he asked.

She struggled to steady her heartbeat. It was hard to believe—even harder to accept—that a man's physical appearance could jangle her nerves. Which was totally ridiculous. She was *not* some teenager in the throes of her first wave of hormones.

"No one tops George when it comes to knowing the ins and

outs of your sport," she replied. "I'm a quick study, so it won't take me long to get up to speed on NASCAR, so to speak."

Keeping his gaze on hers, he slid her card into the pocket of his shirt. "I'll be happy to tutor you privately on all aspects of NASCAR, if that will help."

Her lungs were backing up. She took a careful breath to clear them. She might not know the ins and out of stock car racing, but she was aware that some NASCAR drivers were rumored to have gigantic egos. O'Bryan apparently fell into that category.

"Thanks, but I prefer to use a number of sources when I research a topic." She glanced at her watch. "I don't want to be late for the meeting George scheduled with your boss. After that, I'm off to touch base with your sponsor."

Rafael gave her a thin smile. "Then I'll see you this evening at NSB's employee health fair."

"That's the plan."

He reached for the door, holding it open. "Gil Sizemore's office is on the second floor."

"Thanks." It took a blast of internal strength, but her unsteady legs managed to carry her into the building.

She paused, watching through the glass until he strode out of sight.

"Holy cow," she muttered. She didn't know what it was about him that put her hormones on full alert, but she was going to have to get over it. Control it. It would take more than a handsome face and killer blue eyes to make her forget her purpose for being here, which was to dig into and report on every aspect of Rafael O'Bryan's life.

Caitlin gave her pulse another minute to settle before she turned and headed toward the reception desk and the bank of elevators beyond it.

CHAPTER TWO

THE HOT JUNE DAY had turned into a soft, balmy evening, perfect weather for National Steel Buildings' annual employee health fair and family picnic. The line of people waiting for Rafael's autograph had initially fanned from the table where he sat, snaking between a gazebo illuminated with white twinkle lights and the booths assigned to representatives of various health insurance companies. Located beyond those booths were food kiosks, carnival rides and other entertainment that had been brought in to keep those in attendance amused. As was the gleaming black No. 499 National Steel Buildings stock car parked near the table.

Now, two hours after Rafael had signed his first autograph on a glossy publicity photo, only five people remained lined up in front of him. He'd be the first to admit that his attention wasn't directed at those five fans.

It was the auburn-haired reporter standing a few feet away chatting with Acer Carpenter, NSB's CEO, who held his interest.

It was impossible not to notice that Caitlin Dempsey's lightly tanned skin carried a blush of rose in the evening light. And that her cat-green eyes seemed animated. She'd changed from the sexy black suit and mile-high heels she'd worn earlier into a pair of narrow, aqua cropped pants and a matching sleeveless blouse. Her hair was still gathered back in an intricate French braid.

For an instant, Rafael found himself wondering how many

pins anchored that thick braid. And how long it would take him to loosen them, sending those fire-colored tresses streaming over her shoulders.

He narrowed his eyes at the thought. Not a smart thing to be wondering, considering the sensation that had hit him when he'd barged out the door of Double S Racing and nearly sent her sprawling onto the pavement. For a second, maybe two, while he'd gripped her bare arms to steady her, a sudden burst of heat had sizzled beneath his palms then exploded through his entire body. Bright, hot, sexual heat.

He had felt that same physical desire for other women. But considering his need for secrecy, he would have expected his reaction to have muted the instant Caitlin handed him her business card that identified her as an *investigative* reporter.

It hadn't. So, he'd spent the hours since their encounter cautioning himself that the last thing he needed was to feel any type of physical pull to a woman who'd been hired to dig into his past. A past that he'd spent a great deal of time and effort burying.

Shifting his attention, he signed autographs for the remaining people in line, aware that the freelance photographer *Sports Scene* magazine had hired hovered nearby, snapping photos. When Rafael rose from the table, Acer Carpenter waved him over and extended his hand.

"You're a big hit here tonight, son," declared the middle-aged man who sported a gingery mustache and wire-rim glasses. "I'm calling your boss's office in the morning and have Emma-Lee schedule you to make an appearance at NSB's Christmas party."

"Sounds good." As with every driver on the circuit, Rafael's schedule away from the race track was pretty much at the whim of his major sponsor.

The CEO checked his watch. "Dancing's going to start soon. I'm headed over to the gazebo to make sure our band's got everything they need. I told Caitlin you'd have time now to answer questions." Carpenter delivered a hearty slap to Rafael's shoulder. "I've briefed her on what the board would love to see in the profile, but it's her article. Rafael, I'm counting on you to make sure she gets all the information she needs."

"I'll do my best."

"Caitlin, he's all yours."

As she stepped closer, Rafael caught the faint whiff of a spice-and-flower-scented perfume, and felt his insides tighten. Apparently, his knowing that she was about to spend an inordinate amount of time poking her nose into his business was not enough to blunt his physical reaction to the woman. Just one more complication he didn't need.

"You've been sitting at that table signing autographs for two hours," she said. "How about we walk around while we talk so you can stretch your legs?"

"Works for me." She truly wasn't up to speed on NASCAR if she thought sitting for a couple of hours bothered him. Try spending an entire afternoon strapped and harnessed into his race car's HANS Device.

Her left hand touched a small microphone clipped to the strap of her purse that hung over one shoulder. "I'm going to record our conversation. In a setting like this, it's much easier than trying to jot stuff down."

"Fine," he said, noting that her long, narrow fingers were ringless.

"Do you do this often?" she asked as they strolled by the black-as-pitch No. 499 car.

"Do what?"

"Take your race car to events and sign autographs."

"That isn't my race car."

She craned her neck across her shoulder in the vehicle's direction. "It looks exactly like the one I saw today at Double S Racing."

"True, it does." Rafael noticed the photographer trailing alongside them, snapping an occasional photo. "It isn't even a show car, which is usually a retired race car. This one is an impostor. You're looking at a vehicle painted to exactly resemble the real thing."

"Did you drive it here?"

"No, but I could have because it's street legal. There's no 400-horsepower performance V-8 engine under the hood."

"I spent hours today interviewing your boss, then your crew chief and some of your other team members," she commented as they passed by the gazebo where Acer Carpenter was huddled with the musicians. "They gave me tons of information about the business of racing and NASCAR. No one mentioned impostor cars." She shrugged. "Guess they just scratched the surface."

"There's a lot to learn. And for your information, as far as my schedule is concerned, this gathering isn't an 'event.'"

"In NASCAR lingo, you mean?"

"Exactly. It's a prearranged sponsor appearance, to which National Steel Buildings has invited its employees and some VIP clients."

"Got it. I'll add that to the growing list of things I've learned today. Thanks."

"You're welcome." He'd been cornered by reporters who'd pretended to be expert on all things NASCAR, and some of their questions had been inane. He found Caitlin's honesty about how little she knew refreshing.

They strolled into the area that had been cordoned off for entertainment. A group of people gathered at the Wheel of Fortune, plopping down a dollar for a chance to win more. At another booth, several teenage boys hurled softballs at stacked bottles. From a kiosk around the corner, muffled pops sounded from rifles aimed at a row of moving targets. At the far end of the area, people stood in line to ride the brightly lit Ferris wheel.

The smell of popcorn, grilling meat and cotton candy hung in the air. "Want a lemonade?" Rafael asked when they neared one of the drink booths.

"Yes, thanks."

He made the same offer to the photographer, who declined.

Rafael paid the vendor then handed Caitlin her cup, his fingers brushing hers. Again, he felt it, that jolt. Magnetism. *Heat.* Under the booth's bright lights, she looked gorgeous and appealing. He skimmed his gaze down to her mouth while wondering if she was as elementally aware of him as he was of her.

Either way, that was something he couldn't allow to matter. He had no choice but to deal with her, and he was determined to keep their association on his own terms. Meaning he needed to keep her talking about anything other than himself the majority of the time.

He took a sip of cold, tart lemonade. "My offer to tutor you about NASCAR is still open."

"I might not need those lessons."

"You think you learned everything there is in one afternoon?"

"Hardly. But our readers—and Mr. Carpenter—want this profile to focus on *you*. Racing and NASCAR will probably stay in the background."

"Don't you think *Sports Scene* magazine's readers will be disappointed if you don't give NASCAR equal time?"

Caitlin shook her head. "I think everyone will be disappointed if information about your job overshadows the personal aspects of the profile."

"You should understand that for me, racing is not a job. It's my passion. A part of who I am."

While she studied him over the rim of her cup, her eyes seemed to cool and something settled in their green depths. He realized he was getting his first glimpse of the reporter at work.

"All right, Mr. O'Bryan, let's talk about who you are."

"Since we're going to be together for a number of weeks, I suggest we try something less formal. Call me Rafael. Caitlin's an unusual name." He found he liked the way it sounded when he said it. Soft and feminine and old-fashioned. "Were you named after someone?"

"My grandmother."

His gaze returned to her hair that shined like wet fire under the lights. "Did she have all that flame-colored hair, too?"

Frown lines formed between her brows. "Here's the deal, *Rafael*. I'm the interviewer, not the interviewee. That means I ask the questions."

He shrugged. "Just curious."

"As am I. You were born thirty-four years ago in São Paulo, Brazil, right?"

"Yes." He turned and they began retracing their steps.

"You started racing go-karts in your teens. You were such a natural at the sport you earned the nickname O Tubarão— The Shark—because of the methodical way you went after the competition. Your success in go-karting brought you to the United States when you were barely twenty."

All true. The events that had occurred before he first laid eyes on the go-kart track in São Paulo were what he'd buried deep. "Sounds like you already know all you need to about me."

"Just verifying the information on file. Who taught you to speak English so fluently?"

"A friend."

"In Brazil?"

"Yes."

"How did he or she know English?"

"Her mother was from the States. Texas, I believe."

"Can you give me her name? I'd like to interview some people who knew Rafael O'Bryan back when."

"Her family moved away after she got married. I have no idea what her name is now."

"I'm sure you have other friends in Brazil who would be willing to talk about their famous pal, the NASCAR Sprint Cup Series driver."

"It has been many years since I was in my native country. I've lost contact with people."

"Surely there's some special friend in your past or present whose name you can give me."

"Special friend, meaning lover?"

"You're a sharp guy, Rafael."

He paused, turned to face her. "So sharp that I would never offend a past, present—" He let his voice drift off when the light breeze teased wispy strands of her hair from its fancy braid. Without conscious thought, he reached to tuck the strands back, skimming his fingers over her cheek. *So soft.* He watched emotion glint in her eyes. "—or future lover by giving the media her name," he finished softly.

"What about—" Caitlin cleared her throat "—your own family?"

Just then, a towheaded boy raced up, his right arm covered in a cast from wrist to elbow. He wore baggy shorts and a striped shirt, and clutched a marking pen in his fingers. "Mr. O'Bryan, will you autograph my cast?"

"Sure." Rafael handed Caitlin his cup, then crouched to put himself eye to eye with the boy. He couldn't have timed the interruption better. "What's your name?"

"Bobby. Bobby Watson."

"What happened to your arm?"

"My dumb sister jumped in front of my skateboard. I had to dive off to keep from running over her."

"Sounds like you opted for the best course of action." Out of the corner of his eye, Rafael saw Caitlin gesture to the photographer, who began snapping photos of himself and the boy. "Nevertheless, looks like you had a rough landing."

"Yeah," Bobby agreed, staring wide-eyed at Rafael. "I saw you race once at Homestead."

Rafael raised a brow as he autographed the cast. "How'd I do?"

"You finished second in points for the Chase. Dean Grosso won the championship."

"I seem to remember that." In the final race of the season, he and Grosso had battled it out to the very last lap. Grosso won the NASCAR Sprint Cup Series championship by a hair-raising photo finish.

"Gee, thanks!" the boy exclaimed as he admired the signature.

"You're welcome," Rafael said, returning the marker.

"I gotta go show your autograph to my dumb sister."

Chuckling, Rafael rose as the boy sprinted off.

"Sounds like you've got a big fan," Caitlin commented while handing over his lemonade.

"Not just any fan, but one who knows the lingo. Impressive kid."

They continued retracing their steps, the voices of the people and attractions around them ebbing and fading on the warm air. "Before Bobby showed up, we were talking about your family."

"Were we?"

"I'd like to hear about your parents. Are they in Brazil?"

"Both are deceased."

"Any siblings?"

"No."

"Aunts? Uncles? Cousins?"

He tossed his cup in a trash can they passed. "No."

"You have no family?"

"None to speak of."

She paused, looked up at him. "You really want me to believe you have no friends in Brazil that I can contact?"

"What do you want me to say? It's the truth. Which is how I've answered all your questions. Truthfully."

Sending him a skeptical look, she disposed of her empty cup.

"I'm a man who values his privacy, Caitlin. I've always felt that what I do on my own time is my business."

"After I met with your boss today, he turned me over to his assistant. Emma-Lee Dalton told me that NASCAR Sprint Cup Series drivers and teams spend nearly nine months a year on the road during the racing season. And on any given day a driver can have some sort of activity booked every hour on his schedule."

Rafael saw the same intensity in her green eyes that he heard in her voice. "Your point?"

"Sounds to me like you don't have a lot of time to call your own. And that the majority of your life is centered around NASCAR, which happens to be a very public sport whose participants are expected to stand in a spotlight or anywhere else his major sponsor tells him to."

He took a step forward, dipped his head. "I'll do my best to give you information, Caitlin. What I won't do is fabricate facts about myself just so you can flesh out the profile you're writing."

Her eyes widened. "What are you talking about?"

"You seem to be suspicious because I lack relatives for you to interview. The fact is, my parents were both an only child, so I had no aunts, uncles or cousins. It was just my parents and me." He kept to himself that the mother and father he had no memory of died in an accident when he was barely two years old, leaving him without a single blood relative. To reveal that could link him to the orphanage where he grew up. And put those he most loved in danger.

Rafael glimpsed the man behind the counter in the shooting booth gesturing a tattooed arm. "Hey, buddy, how about buying your lady a couple of chances to hit a target and win a prize?"

Another distraction. Perfect timing. Rafael shifted his gaze back to Caitlin. "Are you game?"

"I've never held a gun."

He raised a brow. *"Never?"*

She shrugged. "My dad doesn't hunt. I have four sisters, we used to play tea party, not cops and robbers."

"Well, you're in luck because I do know how to shoot. I can give you tips."

"Where did you learn to shoot?"

"Brazil has many areas in which to hunt." He left off that he had learned to shoot out of necessity because he'd been considered a vicious man's prey. "This gives you something for your profile that links back to my native country."

"And since those links are apparently rare, I'd better not pass up this opportunity."

He grinned at the sardonic tone in her voice. "My thoughts, exactly." He snagged her wrist, easing her through the crowd. Pulling a few bills out of his pocket, he handed them to the man behind the counter. "How many shots will that buy?"

"Five."

Blowing out a breath, Caitlin accepted the rifle from the vendor. "All right, Wyatt Earp, I'm ready for your tips."

"Don't aim."

She blinked. "I thought the object was to hit the target."

"True. The thing is, most people are accurate in pointing at something, but when they try to aim a weapon the mechanics of doing so somehow interfere with that natural ability."

"Just point? Don't aim?"

"You got it."

She raised the rifle, rested its butt against one shoulder, then jerked the trigger.

"Missed the entire target!" the man behind the counter announced.

Caitlin sent Rafael a withering look. "Some teacher you are. Maybe you'd better stick to driving a race car."

"Like everything, shooting takes practice." He stepped behind her, put his hands on her shoulders. Her blouse was sleeveless, so his palms settled against bare skin. *Creamy, bare skin that stirred his blood.*

She instantly stiffened and whipped her head around. "What are you doing?"

"Giving you another tip. In racing, I don't drive the car using just the steering wheel. I use my entire body. The same thing applies to firing a weapon." He slid his arms around her, closed his hands over hers where they lay against the rifle. Instantly, electricity coursed from her fingers straight to his gut. If she felt it, too, he couldn't tell. Surely this hunger that was crawling around inside him wasn't all one-sided.

In his peripheral vision, Rafael saw that a handful of people had stopped to watch them. The photographer moved around, shooting pictures from different angles.

Refocusing his attention, Rafael made a few minute adjustments in her grip. "Lean against me," he urged. "Just relax."

"Relax?" Was it his imagination, or had her voice gone hoarse? With the noise from the crowd and the rides, he couldn't be sure.

"Relax," he repeated, shifting his body against hers to assume the correct stance. Her spine remained stiff while her seductive scent pulsed off her warm flesh in little waves, clogging his lungs.

"Don't jerk the trigger," he murmured against her cheek. Without thinking, without being able to think, he tightened his arms around her and battled the urge to keep from burying his face in all that flame-red hair. "Just squeeze. Gently."

The instant the rifle fired, she surged from his hold.

"You hit the target this time, missy."

"I'm done," Caitlin said, almost shoving the rifle into the vendor's hands.

"Your gentleman friend paid for three more tries." The man swept a tattooed arm in the direction of the stuffed animals hanging over the targets. "You get lucky, you could go home with a prize."

"No, thanks." She turned to Rafael. Her face was flushed, her eyes glittering. Her pulse tripped wildly in the hollow of her throat. Oh, yeah, he'd gotten to her.

"I have enough info for tonight." As she spoke, she gestured for the photographer. "I'll see you tomorrow," she added before she and the photographer strode off together.

Rafael tracked her until she disappeared into the crowd. To his disgust, he realized he was anticipating seeing her again far more than any man should whose very life might depend on keeping the secrets that she was trying to uncover hidden.

THE CHASE for the NASCAR Sprint Cup. Pole position. Banking. Drafting. Tight versus loose. When it came to NASCAR, there were a kazillion terms to learn, Caitlin thought three days later while easing into a corner of one of the garage bays at the Pennsylvania race track.

It was Saturday, and the final hour of practice was about to begin.

Centered in the bay beneath a row of fluorescent lights

was the gleaming black No. 499 car. The real one this time, with massive red and white National Steel Buildings decals on the back, sides and top of the hood. The hood was raised while several members of the garage crew wearing team polo shirts and dark pants peered at the engine. Another—the *tire specialist*—was squatted down, conducting an intense examination of the car's right front tire.

On the far side of the car, crew chief Denton Moss stood with several team members. All of them except for Rafael wore similar Double S Racing apparel.

O Tubarão—The Shark—had suited up in his black uniform covered in sponsorship logos, his dark hair mussed from wearing a helmet during the day's practice sessions. Standing amid his teammates, Rafael looked like a prime example of raw male power. Adding to the drool factor was the way the snug fit of his uniform emphasized the contours of his strong shoulders and flat belly.

Even now, Caitlin couldn't think about their session at the shooting booth without feeling a little flutter in her belly. The way he'd wrapped his arms around her, steadying the rifle she held while he whispered target-shooting tips in that tantalizing deep, accented voice had turned her insides upside down.

Just thinking about that reaction had her gritting her teeth. She was not proud of it. Determined not to repeat it. An investigative reporter did *not* get weak in the knees over an interviewee. Which was all Mr. Rafael O'Bryan was. Emotionally, she was not in trouble. Period.

It had become crystal clear at the health fair that he did not intend for her to learn anything more about him than he wanted her to know. Which left no doubt that if she didn't change her tactics, she would have scant information on what personal issues defined the man by the time the assignment wrapped up. Which was why, the following day, she had approached him as someone he could tutor, not as a reporter intent on laying open his past.

Since then, Rafael had answered every question she had lobbed at him about NASCAR. It wasn't her imagination that he was getting more comfortable around her. Less wary.

Soon, she would again focus her questions on his personal life. In the meantime, she was enjoying learning about the sport that only days before had been a blank slate in her mind.

"I love this smell."

Caitlin glanced at the woman who walked up beside her. "You mean car exhaust and smoking tires?"

"You got it," Emma-Lee Dalton said with a grin. Like Caitlin, Gil Sizemore's blonde, blue-eyed assistant was dressed in a long-sleeved blouse and slim jeans, security credentials dangling from a lanyard around her neck. "Comes from growing up with parents who are huge NASCAR fans. They toted my sisters and me to almost every race each season."

Caitlin had taken an instant liking to Emma-Lee. Which was a good thing, since a reservation glitch had landed them in the same room in a nearby hotel that was filled to the max.

"I guess those particular smells take getting used to," Caitlin commented.

"Guess so." Emma-Lee cocked her head. "How are your interviews with members of Rafael's team going?"

"Like a well-rehearsed play." Caitlin heard the frustration in her voice that had been building inside her for days. Since she'd switched the focus to NASCAR when she was with Rafael, she had planned to learn personal aspects about him from interviews with his teammates. Things were not going as expected.

"Are some of the team members not cooperating?"

"Just the opposite." Caitlin raised her voice to be heard over the high-pitched whir of an air wrench. "Every person

I've asked about Rafael has given me the same basic information."

"Such as?"

"'O'Bryan's a scary good driver. He represents a constant threat to his competitors. He makes a point to treat his team with respect.'" Caitlin eased out a breath. "Everyone seems willing to talk my ear off about what type of driver Rafael is. But when it comes to the in-depth what-makes-this-guy-tick type of information, I get zilch."

"Rafael's one of those guys who likes his privacy."

Both women took an instant step back to avoid a team member darting past them.

"There aren't many people close to him," Emma-Lee added.

"Our readers—and NSB—aren't going to be happy if the profile I turn in only touches the surface of who he is. I imagine he also likes having a sponsor."

"I see what you mean." Emma-Lee tapped a finger against her pursed lips. "Two years ago, Rafael drove for another racing team. I heard about him helping one of his teammates who was also from South America. I think a member of the guy's family had some sort of medical problem."

"How did Rafael help?"

"Used his influence to cut through red tape. I think. Like I said, it was two years ago and I'm vague on the details."

"Do you know who the man is that Rafael helped?"

"No, but I can find out from Rue."

"Rue?"

"Rue Larrabee, owner of the Cut 'N' Chat Beauty Salon. The wife of the guy Rafael helped is…or was one of Rue's clients."

Caitlin smiled. At last she might be getting somewhere.

"In fact," Emma-Lee continued, "why don't you plan to go with me to the Tuesday Tarts. I'll introduce you to Rue."

"Tuesday Tarts?"

"It's a group of gals who get together on Tuesday nights to schmooze and gossip. The membership is loose-knit, so we never know who's going to show up. But whoever's there might be able to add some information about Rafael that doesn't have to do with his driving." Emma-Lee tapped a few buttons on her cell phone, checked the display. "I can't make the next meeting, but I'll be at the following one."

"I'll join you. Where do you meet?"

"The back room of Maudie's Down Home Diner. You've been there, right?"

"No."

"You've got to make time to go to Maudie's. It's like a small-town café for the racing community. We can all kick back and relax and just be ourselves. Rafael goes there a lot. He could take you." Emma-Lee glanced at her watch. "I have to track down my boss and make sure he knows what's on his schedule for this evening. I'll call you when I get the guy's name from Rue."

"Thanks." Caitlin shifted her attention back to the activity in the garage. The car's hood was now closed and the tire specialist was out of sight.

Denton Moss, the headset he would use to communicate when the noise level turned deafening hanging half on and half off one side of his head, stood near the driver's door, talking to Rafael. His expression serious, Rafael said a few words, then turned toward the car. For a split second, his gaze met Caitlin's...then lowered to focus on her lips. Raw emotion glinted in his eyes.

Longings, needs she'd thought she'd finished with years ago, sprang out fresh and strong. Something deep inside her wanted to give way to them and feel again. Just feel.

In the next heartbeat, Rafael shifted his gaze, then climbed through the window of his car.

Hoping her unsteady legs would continue to support her, Caitlin turned away. Then squeezed her eyes shut. Oh, Lord, she was in trouble.

The car's starter chugged, then the boom of all eight pistons roared through the garage. She wasn't sure which was louder—the engine or the pounding of her heart.

Big. Trouble.

CHAPTER THREE

ON THE MONDAY EVENING after the Pennsylvania race, the air inside Maudie's Down Home Diner was ripe with its usual delicious smells. Every chrome-trimmed red-vinyl-covered stool along the length of the counter was occupied. As were most of the red-vinyl-upholstered booths that jutted out from each wall and the tables crowding the black-and-white-checkered floor.

Rafael strode toward the rear of the diner past framed photographs of NASCAR drivers, both present and past. He considered himself lucky when he claimed the last vacant booth.

He checked his watch, noting *he* was on time. But there was no sign of the woman who'd called and asked him to meet her there.

Caitlin Dempsey. At the Pocono track, he'd been acutely aware of her, hovering in the periphery of the garage, then the pit stall. But qualifying, practice and several sponsor commitments had kept him so busy he'd barely had time to speak to her. He'd thought about her, though. Too much. Then there was the dream in which he'd returned to his motor home late at night and found her waiting for him in the moonlight. The dream had quickly turned erotic when he'd tugged her inside and ravaged her mouth with his own. He'd jolted awake to an empty bed. The furious frustration pulsing through his system had kept him awake the remainder of the night. And dogged him the day of the race.

He stabbed his fingers through his hair. Never before had he allowed thoughts of a woman to interfere with his racing. If his crew chief, Denton Moss, found out his mind hadn't been entirely in the game that past weekend, he would skin him alive.

What, Rafael wondered, was it about this one particular woman that pulled at him? It wasn't just physical, he was sure of that. There was some emotion in the mix. But, what?

No answer was forthcoming. Not even when he spotted Caitlin threading her way between the tables and that instant magnetism tightened his gut.

His gaze swept down her, then up. She was wearing snug jeans and a vibrant green blouse that hugged her lean body. He took an instant to appreciate her walk that gave an elegant sort of swing to her denim-clad hips. But his attention riveted on the way her long hair draped across her shoulders like skeins of copper silk.

How many times had he imagined himself unplaiting the braid she perpetually wore? Now, here she was with that mass of hair long and free and about to be within touching distance. All he wanted was to bury his face in it.

"Sorry I'm late."

He shut down his thoughts with a silent curse as she scooted in opposite him. She posed a danger to what he held most dear, and the main thought in his brain was getting his hands on her. Not smart. "No problem. I've been here only a few minutes."

She looked around, her mouth curving. "So, this is Maudie's. Emma-Lee said it was the equivalent of a 1950s small-town café where everyone connected to racing comes to kick back and relax." Caitlin remet his gaze. "She said you eat here a lot."

"Food's good." He could smell her perfume now, dark and tempting. "The atmosphere's secondary."

A slender young waitress with short black hair appeared with glasses of water and menus sheathed in plastic. "Welcome back, Mr. O'Bryan."

"Good to be back. Mellie, this is Caitlin Dempsey. It's her first time at Maudie's."

The pretty young waitress grinned. "After you taste the food, it won't be the last."

"That's what I hear," Caitlin commented.

"Has the diner been this busy all night?" Rafael asked.

"Yes, and we're short on help. I bet by the time I crawl into bed, I'll hear my feet crying."

"No doubt," he agreed. "How's your little one?"

"Wonderful. Lily's upstairs in my apartment with Al's wife. Speaking of Al, his meat loaf is tonight's special. We've had a run on it and there's only one pan left."

Caitlin handed her menu back to Mellie. "I'm sold."

"Make it two."

"I must be losing my perspective," Caitlin commented after Mellie moved off.

"Why's that?"

"Mellie doesn't look old enough to have a baby."

"I thought the same thing the first time she had Lily down here on one of her breaks. Lily's two years old, so I guess Mellie got an early start on motherhood."

"Is she raising her on her own? That must be hard."

"As far as I know. But Mellie is a hard worker, and seeing her with Lily is amazing." Rafael shifted against the upholstered bench, refocused his thoughts on the green-eyed woman sitting opposite him. It hadn't been lost on him that, after the health fair, she'd kept the focus of her questions on NASCAR. Its rules. Terms. The tactics he used on the track. He had no idea why she'd changed her strategy, but the less personal questions she lobbed his way, the better. To his surprise, he'd found he enjoyed sharing his knowledge with a woman who seemed to be developing a genuine enthusiasm for the sport he loved.

It was time now to find out why she had called him to meet her here. "On the phone you said you have more questions. About racing?"

"*Related* to it. At Pocono, I noticed several drivers doing things that benefit certain charities. Some even have established their own foundations. I checked, and couldn't find anything about you having an official connection to either."

"I don't." He'd taken steps to ensure that no one could track what he did with the majority of his winnings. Tension coiled through his spine at the thought she had stumbled onto something. "That isn't a requirement."

"No, it's not." Caitlin paused only long enough for Mellie to deliver plates of piping-hot meat loaf and vegetables, then hurry off to take another order. "What is it with you, O'Bryan?"

He picked up his fork. "What do you mean?"

"You did something that would give your fans a glimpse of the man behind the sneaky good driver, but you kept it quiet."

"You think I'm a sneaky good driver?"

She gave him a withering look. "Does the name Hector Jonas ring a bell?"

"Sure. He's a jackman on a team I used to drive for."

"He's also the guy whose baby niece in Ecuador needed open-heart surgery to save her life. He's got a wife and three kids of his own, and didn't have extra money to send home to chip in for the operation. He told me that when you heard about his niece, you contacted the doctor in Ecuador and arranged to pay for everything. Even flew Hector and his family there."

"He's a good man." Rafael jerked a shoulder. "Loyal."

"Very. At first, Hector hemmed and hawed when I tried to get him to talk about what you did for his family."

"Amazing, isn't it, how some people just don't want their personal business made public." Rafael sipped the iced tea he'd ordered with his meal. Since there was nothing to connect what he'd done for the Jonas family to his activities in Brazil, the tightness in his shoulders had begun to ease. He was actually starting to enjoy himself. "So, what did you do to force Hector to talk? Use some sort of reporter torture technique?"

"I was just about to pull out my whip when his wife showed up," Caitlin answered, her voice mirroring his sardonic tone. "She was more than willing to chat about your generosity. To hear her talk, you should be made a saint."

"A little girl needed help. I was in the position to give it, that's all."

"*All?* What you did was huge." Caitlin wagged her fork at him before she scooped up another bite of meat loaf. "Look, I understand you feel that what you do when you're not on the race track is solely your business."

"It is."

"I'm not here to debate that. Hector's story is going in the profile. I thought you might want to verify the details. Give me a quote or two. At the very least, we could discuss your philanthropy."

"We just did. Nothing more to say."

She laid her fork aside, frustration written all over her face. "Maybe I should use my whip on you."

He hooked a brow. "This conversation has suddenly turned very interesting."

While she rolled her eyes, he glanced toward the front of the diner. Half the stools at the counter were now vacant, and only a few customers lingered in the booths and tables. Movement at the front door caught his eye in time for him to see Bart Branch, a NASCAR Sprint Cup Series driver for PDQ Racing, step inside.

"Want to meet the winner of yesterday's race?"

Caitlin's gaze followed his. "His last name is Branch, right?"

"Right. That's Bart. His twin, Will, is also a driver."

"I overheard some team members at the race track talking about a man named Hilton Branch. Something about embezzling money. Any relation?"

"Bart and Will's father. He was a banker who owned the race team his sons drove for. Money got tight, so he embezzled from his bank, then went on the run when things started falling apart. He's in prison now."

Rafael waved Mellie over and asked her to invite Bart to join them. Seconds later, the tall, blond-haired driver with the cocky grin stood beside the booth. After introducing him to Caitlin, Bart shook her hand while she congratulated him on his first-place finish the previous day.

"Thanks." Bart met Rafael's gaze. "Too bad about your engine trouble."

"Yeah," Rafael agreed. It had slowed him in the opening phase of the race. The needed carburetor adjustment had cost him precious laps and put him at the end of the pack. By the close of the race, he'd run out of time to maneuver his way farther forward than ninth place. "I plan to do better in Michigan."

"Not if I can help it." Grinning, Bart angled his head toward the front of the diner. "I've got a stool and a hot cup of coffee waiting for me at the counter. Nice to meet you, Caitlin."

"Same here," she said, her gaze tracking the driver as he strolled off. "Interesting."

"What is?"

"Bart's got a stool reserved at the counter, which is where Mellie spends a fair amount of time, dropping off order slips, then picking up food. He kept glancing at her while he chatted with us. Think maybe there's some chemistry going on there?"

"Could be." Rafael narrowed his gaze. "Do you ever just get off the clock? Stop trying to figure out what's going on in other people's lives?"

"Delving into what makes certain people tick isn't a nine-to-five job." She shrugged. The movement waterfalled her thick hair over her shoulders. "I sometimes learn a lot more from watching what people do than listening to their words."

"Because some of the words are lies?"

"Oftentimes. But actions usually always tell the truth."

This, he thought, was a reminder of just how perceptive she was. And how careful he needed to be around her. "Any more questions for me tonight?"

"No," Caitlin answered. "I'm going back to the hotel to polish my notes on the interview with Hector Jonas and his wife. This is your last chance to expand your comments on what you did for that family."

"I'll pass. Speaking of family, at the health fair you mentioned your four sisters. Where do you fit in?"

"I'm the oldest."

"The mature one."

"So I'd like to think."

"Where did you grow up?"

"Oklahoma City."

"Do you still live there?"

"My family does. I relocated to New York City when I went to work for the magazine." She paused, then scowled. "And now you know more about me than I do about you. That's plain sad."

Grinning, he swept the check off the table just as she reached for it. "Actually, it's very interesting."

"I invited you here, I should pay," Caitlin said as they

walked toward the front counter where Bart Branch was settled on a stool, chatting with the dark-haired waitress.

"So, Mellie," Bart said, "you haven't told me where you and Lily are from."

Mellie opened her mouth to reply, but closed it when a woman who Rafael recognized as the cook's wife stepped out of the swinging door that led to the kitchen. In her arms she held a bright-eyed, dark-haired little girl who squealed when she spotted him.

"Rafaaaeel!"

"There's my girl." He looked at Mellie. "Okay if I hold Lily for a minute?"

Something close to relief flickered in Mellie's eyes. "I doubt she'll let you leave unless you do."

The toddler was already reaching for him when he swung her into his arms. Her tiny hands gripping his shirt collar, she bounced in the crook of his elbow, her pretty, rosy-cheeked face alight with joy.

He'd grown up in the orphanage, often taking care of the younger kids. Now, being around children was as natural for him as breathing.

Though he could decipher only half her chatter, he gave Lily a solemn nod as she continued to bounce in his arms.

When a cell phone chimed, Caitlin dug in her purse. She glanced at her phone's display. "My editor," she said, then moved off to answer the call.

"Editor?" Mellie asked. "Is Caitlin a writer?"

"Reporter," Rafael said while softly pinching Lily's cheek. She squealed in delight, her grasp on his shirt tightening.

"A reporter?"

"*Investigative* reporter for *Sports Scene* magazine," Rafael added.

When Mellie continued to stare at Caitlin, Bart placed

a forearm on the counter and leaned in. "Mellie, are you okay?"

"Yes. Yes." She turned, lifted a coffeepot off the warmer and refilled Bart's cup. "I... At one time I thought I might want to be a reporter."

"Glad that didn't happen," Bart said. "Otherwise, you wouldn't have wound up here at Maudie's."

Watching the exchange, Rafael had to agree that Caitlin was right. He could almost see the chemistry in the air surrounding the waitress and the NASCAR Sprint Cup Series driver.

Rafael glanced sideways when he heard Caitlin end her phone call. He could read her well enough now so that he knew the sharpness in her green eyes meant her reporter's radar had snapped back on.

Instantly, the tenseness resettled in his shoulders. Had something her editor said clued her in to the truth about his past?

With paranoia tickling at the edges of his rational mind, he handed Lily back to her babysitter, then laid the check and some bills on the counter.

"I'll walk you to your car," he said as he swung the door open for Caitlin.

"That'd be good," she said. "Because I suddenly have a couple more questions to ask you."

"YOU MUST HAVE SPENT time around small children to be so good with them."

Caitlin made the observation as she and Rafael stepped out of Maudie's into the warm June night. Watching Lily giggle with delight while in Rafael's arms had given Caitlin insight into a totally unexpected—and immensely compelling—side of the man.

Which was her bad luck. The last thing she needed was one more reason to find O Tubarão so appealing.

"A natural gift," Rafael commented.

Moonlight poured down, mingling with the reflection from the security lights guarding the parking lot on one side of Maudie's diner. "Does that mean you haven't spent a lot of time around small children?"

"I have no children of my own, so I suppose not."

She stopped beside her rental car, turned to face him. The pale light seemed to add slivers of silver to his Viking-blue eyes.

"While Lily was bouncing in your arms, she held on for dear life to your shirt collar."

"So?"

"So, I saw the scar on your chest. Rafael, it looks long and jagged and seems dangerously close to your heart. What happened to you?"

"An accident."

"Really?" she asked, sarcasm slashing her voice. "I thought maybe you'd gotten your chest sliced open on purpose."

He slid his hands into the pockets of his slacks. "Wouldn't be a lot of sense in that."

Feeling her frustration level kick up a notch, she unlocked the car's door, pulled it open and tossed her purse onto the seat. Squaring her shoulders, she turned back. "I intend to write the most thorough and comprehensive profile of you that I can. With or without your cooperation. You do understand that, don't you?"

"Of course."

"Then why won't you talk to me?"

"I've been talking to you for days."

"About NASCAR. Racing." The wind picked up, whipping her hair against her cheek. She swept a hand beneath the long mass and scooped it across one shoulder. "Not about yourself. Not about growing up in Brazil."

He took a step forward, boxing her in between his body and the car door. The thrill that sprinted straight up her spine irritated her. "What do you think you're doing?"

"Getting ready to tell you something about my native country. Did you know that Brazil is considered to be the most romantic place on earth?"

"That factoid got right by me."

"Too bad. You see, Brazilians have perfected the art of kissing." Keeping his eyes locked on hers, he reached out, caught a lock of her hair and toyed with it gently.

With his hand so near her face, Caitlin's throat tightened. She was dry kindling and this gorgeous Latin-Irish hunk was a blowtorch. She wasn't sure what would happen if he touched her.

Just the prospect that he might sent heat creeping up the back of her neck. "Well, thanks for that info. I need to get back to my hotel room and work on my notes."

Slowly, he twined her hair around his fingers. "Would you like a demonstration?"

His voice had lowered, its accented tone infuriatingly sexy. His hand was so close to her cheek now, she could feel the heat from his skin.

"No, thanks. Turns out, I've been kissed before."

"I don't doubt it. Nor do I doubt that, if it's your wish, you'll be kissed again." He skimmed his gaze down to her mouth. "Very soon."

Inside she went still as his hands slid beneath her hair and slowly folded around the nape of her neck. His palms were warm and heavy against her skin. She could feel the strength in him but sensed the control. The combination was electrifying.

His thumbs moved gently just behind her ears. He eased her

head back slightly and lowered his mouth to within a whisper of hers.

"What is your wish, Caitlin?"

She knew she should step back. Tell him she wasn't interested. But, dammit, she didn't want to step back. Because she *was* interested.

Going with impulse, she raised on tiptoe to graze her lips across his. "This," she murmured.

When he settled his mouth on hers, every muscle in her body went lax. His kiss wasn't demanding, it wasn't urgent. It was devastating.

With a moan of pleasure, she slid her fingers into his dark hair and fisted there. His mouth was so tempting, his taste so enticing.

He deepened the kiss, his lips slanting across hers. Excitement sparked along every nerve ending. Flames erupted beneath her flesh, fierce and intense.

A sense of urgency pulsed through her when his hands settled on her hips.

"I've been wondering what it would be like to kiss you," he murmured against her throat. "How you would taste. I was going crazy waiting to find out."

She'd been going crazy herself.

"Kissing isn't the only thing I've been thinking about doing with you." One of his hands lifted, tunneled through her hair. The other moved over the curve of her hip.

She felt his fingers slide beneath the hem of her blouse as he gazed down at her, his eyes gleaming in the moonlight. "I want to make love with you, Caitlin. Come home with me. Tonight."

The huskiness that had settled in his voice had her knees going weak. She didn't just want to go home with him, she wanted to shove him into her car and race, NASCAR-style, to get there.

And that was just crazy. Totally wrong. A small whisper of sanity told her she had no business forgetting her purpose here in this sudden crazy desire to be with this man.

"I... I can't." She tried with little success to catch her breath. Every pulse point in her body felt like a jackhammer.

When he made no move to release her, she pulled back. And felt the slide of his fingers against her flesh as his hand eased from beneath her blouse.

Her heart and lungs were straining. She had no control over them. No control over the ache of wanting that was so huge it left little room for reason. That knowledge shot a dazed fear into her system. Years ago, a man whom she thought she could trust without question had the same stunning effect on her. Then he'd betrayed her. As a result, the career she loved had been put on the line and her heart broken.

She had vowed then she would never again take anyone at face value. Never again trust so freely. Yet, here she was, close to jumping into bed with a man she hardly knew. A man who had no intention of opening up to her and allowing her to see what was below the surface.

Never again.

"I...we shouldn't be doing this." Her voice—her entire body—quaked.

"It's something we both want, is it not?"

Instead of answering, she curled her fingers into her palms until her nails bit into her flesh. "I'm on a job. *You're* the job. I'm supposed to be a professional. Dammit, I *am* a professional."

"There's no question about that."

"There would be, if I slept with you." She dragged in a deep breath. "I encouraged you to kiss me, and I shouldn't have. I can't do this, Rafael. I just can't."

He gazed down at her for a long moment. "Your choice, Caitlin. Believe it or not, seducing a woman in a parking lot isn't my usual style." He shifted his gaze, staring into the darkness. "You...change things," he said when he looked back at her. "Not all change is good. Perhaps it's wise not to take this any further."

"I...think so."

"I'll see you tomorrow, then."

"Yes."

She slid into her car and watched him stride away in the silver moonlight while regret filled the air around her like invisible smoke.

CHAPTER FOUR

RAFAEL'S CREW CHIEF, Denton Moss, had decided to try some new adjustments on the No. 499 car, in the hopes of avoiding the carburetor problems that had cost them laps at last weekend's race. So the following days had been spent running speed and engine tests. Tweaks were still being made after the car rolled off the big hauler on Thursday at the speedway in Michigan.

The intense consulting with his crew chief, his car chief, his engine specialist and various other members of his team had taken up the majority of Rafael's time. Through it all, he'd had little opportunity to think about Caitlin, much less see her. Which suited him just fine.

Now that the heat of need no longer fired his blood, he could admit that kissing her had been a mistake. A big one. Always before, it had been easy to view relationships with women as temporary encounters. No strings. No emotional involvement. No reason to reveal anything but surface information about himself. But where the redheaded reporter was concerned, he instinctively knew he could fall hard. So hard, it would be impossible not to want to open up and share parts of himself that he had never before even considered confiding in another woman. Including the truth about his past.

Which could turn into a deadly mistake.

So, in the days since he'd stood with her in that moonlight-drenched parking lot, he had forced himself to take an emotional step back. Resolved to concentrate all his thoughts and effort on his driving.

Inside his helmet, the radio receiver crackled to life. "Rafael, can you hear me? Talk to me, man."

The voice belonged to Yancy, his spotter. Rafael tightened his gloved hands on the steering wheel. So much for keeping his mind on his job. Even though his thoughts about Caitlin had taken only seconds, it was not advisable to lose his focus while racing three-wide along the backstretch at 170 miles an hour. Not if he intended to win this race and deliver the checkered flag for Double S Racing.

Which he did.

"I hear you, Yancy. What's it look like?"

"The No. 475 and No. 515 are coming up on your rear. Gotta keep low or they'll get by you."

"Trying." Bart Branch was in the No. 475 car. One of Rafael's teammates, Ben Edmonds, drove the other.

Rafael maintained his speed, hugging the inside groove until he felt his own car about to lose traction. Reluctantly, he eased up on the gas, just enough to maintain control.

When he shot out of the next turn, a plume of smoke up ahead instantly caught his attention. He knew from experience that the smoke signaled a blown engine on one of the lead cars.

In the following seconds, everything changed.

The wind billowed dark smoke across a section of the track. Cars began skidding haphazardly as oil spewed from the damaged vehicle.

"Rafael, stay low," Yancy shouted. "Stay low. Keep going."

On blind faith, Rafael did as instructed, having no choice but to drive into the acrid cloud of smoke. Then his luck ran out. A car to his right fishtailed, hit the outside wall, then careened off of it. The car T-boned Rafael's directly in the passenger side.

The hard impact rattled his teeth. Air blasted from his lungs. Another car plowed into him from behind. Instinct took over as he fought to keep his skidding car from flipping.

Too late, he thought as his car went airborne, then barrel rolled onto the infield.

CAITLIN AND EMMA-LEE DALTON had just made their way into the garage when the earthshaking roar of forty-three V-8s racing around the speedway's track fell silent. The sudden cessation of noise had Caitlin halting midstep. "What just happened?"

"Bad news. When it gets suddenly quiet during a race, that means there's a wreck."

Caitlin saw the team members drop what they were doing and crowd around the TV screens they used to keep up to date on the race. She and Emma-Lee squeezed into the group watching the nearest screen.

"...caused by oil on the track," the track announcer was saying as the camera panned across wrecked and smoking race cars. "Eight cars are involved." He proceeded to give the car numbers and each driver's name, ending with "...the No. 499 National Steel Buildings car driven by Rafael O'Bryan. It looks like it sustained the most damage. O'Bryan's the only driver who has yet to climb out onto the track."

Staring at the mangled vehicle, Caitlin felt her chest tighten until she could barely breathe.

"We hope O'Bryan's not hurt," the announcer continued. "His car's done for the day, that's for sure."

Caitlin clenched her fists as she watched smoke roll from under the hood of Rafael's car. "Is..." Her throat had gone so dry that her voice sounded like a rusty rasp. "Is there a way to find out...if Rafael's hurt?"

Emma-Lee glanced at Caitlin, did a double take and clamped a hand on her arm. "Hey, you're as pale as a sheet. You'd better sit down."

"I'm okay." Caitlin kept her eyes on the monitor. The drivers who had already emerged from their own cars were heading toward the black No. 499 car. Thousands of fans in the stands fell silent while emergency workers and a couple of members of Rafael's pit crew arrived at the wreck simultaneously.

They converged en masse on the driver's side of the car. For Caitlin, time seemed to expand while the men huddled together. *Let Rafael be okay,* she prayed. *Please, let him be okay.*

In what looked like a synchronized move, the men all stepped back and the window net went down. Rafael's gloved hand gave a thumbs-up sign to the silent crowd. Moments later, he eased himself out of the window, then tugged off his helmet.

"Folks, it looks like O'Bryan's okay." The announcer's voice was barely audible over the cheers that erupted from the crowd.

Only when Emma-Lee's cell phone pinged did she release her grip on Caitlin's arm. "Gil's up in the suite with Acer Carpenter," Emma-Lee read off the phone's display. She flipped down its cover, then remet Caitlin's gaze. "I need to head up there to coordinate some stuff for Gil. Are you okay?"

"Yes. Of course." Caitlin shoved her heavy braid off her shoulder. Only then did she realize her hands her trembling, just like her legs. "I just…" She wasn't sure what emotions were churning inside her, and she needed time to sort them out. "This is the first wreck I've seen during a race. I didn't realize…"

Emma-Lee nodded slowly. "Yeah, they're scary." As if she possessed a window on Caitlin's emotions, Emma-Lee reached out, squeezed her hand. "No matter if Rafael's hurt or not, he has to take an ambulance ride to the Infield Care Center to get checked out. When he's released from the ICC, he'll get swarmed by the media. Everyone will want to hear about the race from his perspective."

The heavy thrum of engines suddenly resumed as cars that had not been as seriously damaged began to make their way back to the garages for repairs in hopes of finishing the race.

Emma-Lee leaned in to be heard. "After that, I expect Rafael will head to his motor home to change clothes, then find the nearest helicopter so he can get to the airport and fly home."

"Won't he need to meet with his team? Maybe with Gil?"

"Sure, but that'll happen back at headquarters, especially since the wreck wasn't caused by a part failure or driver error on this team." Emma-Lee lifted a brow. "I can set it up if you want to hitch a ride back to Charlotte with Rafael."

"No." Caitlin dragged in a deep breath. "I have an interview scheduled in a half hour with a former crew chief who was on the first racing team Rafael joined when he arrived in the States. I don't know how long that will take. I'll just fly home later with the team, as planned."

"Sounds good. The race will probably get red flagged for a bit while the track is cleaned of oil and debris. I'll hook up with you later."

Emma-Lee walked off just as a tow truck pulled up with what was left of the No. 499 car.

Caitlin caught sight of mangled metal an instant before the team members swarmed around the vehicle. With the garage nearly empty, she was thankful to have some space to herself for a few moments. Time to get her system settled.

And maybe sort out what the heck had just happened inside her.

A man she'd known barely two weeks had been involved in a crash. Considering he could have been seriously hurt, the sharp concern she'd felt for his well-being was understandable.

What wasn't so easy to explain was the way her heart had clenched. Was *still* clenched. And that she'd had to control an almost frenzied need to dash out onto the track and check on Rafael herself.

Those emotions should not be experienced by a professional, impartial journalist. Which, she conceded, she no longer was when it came to Rafael O'Bryan. After all, the man had kissed her brainless, prompting her to seriously consider—at least for a few seconds—sleeping with him. Hard to remain impartial after all that.

She'd been nothing but relieved in the days since then that Rafael had made no mention of the kiss that set her off like a California brush fire. He'd gone about his business while she continued to conduct research and interviews for the profile. And worked very hard not to let herself think about that kiss. Or the fact he had admitted she had changed things.

Which had been an effort in futility. Because she had thought about all that. A lot.

Now, it was suddenly crystal clear that what she felt was more than just physical. Somehow, someway, she'd become involved with Rafael on an emotional level, as well. On more than one level, it seemed.

This man, who was such an enigma to her, mattered. *He mattered.*

"Wonderful," she muttered. How the hell was she going to handle this? As a professional journalist? As a woman?

Caitlin stood by herself in the noisy garage for several long minutes, waiting for answers.

They never came.

"WELCOME TO THE Tuesday Tarts," Rue Larrabee said as Caitlin stepped into a back room of Maudie's diner.

"Glad to be here."

The diner wouldn't close until ten and the scent of delicious homemade meals lingered in the room that was sectioned off into two distinct areas. One had metal shelves loaded with canned goods and sacks of flour and other staples. Additional shelves held massive stainless-steel bowls, stacks of hand towels and freshly laundered aprons.

The second area looked more like a sitting room with a scattering of love seats mixed with upholstered chairs. A table covered with a crisp white cloth held a coffeemaker, mugs and trays filled with a variety of scrumptious-looking desserts.

By Caitlin's guesstimate, ten women had already made themselves comfortable on the love seats and chairs. One of them was Emma-Lee, who grinned from her spot beside Mellie, the young, dark-haired waitress who was off work already. Mellie's two-year-old daughter had fallen asleep on Emma-Lee's lap.

Caitlin looked back at Rue. "Emma-Lee assured me the group is used to having drop-ins."

"Oh, honey, we are." Rue Larrabee was a tall, attractive woman with flaming-red hair. "It's a rare Tuesday night when we don't have a guest. In fact, I've invited a client from my beauty shop to drop by tonight. She should be here soon."

Rue put a light hand on Caitlin's arm. "Let's get you some refreshments."

"I'll just have coffee for now," Caitlin said as they moved to the table. "No dessert."

Rue's gaze swept up and down Caitlin. "You have more willpower than me, which is why you have such a gorgeous figure." Rue snagged a mug off the table while saying, "Emma-Lee told me you're a reporter for *Sports Scene* magazine, writing an article on one of Double S Racing's Sprint Cup Series drivers. She didn't mention which driver."

"Rafael O'Bryan," Caitlin said as she accepted the mug filled with piping-hot coffee.

Instant concern settled in Rue's eyes. "I watched Sunday's race on TV. My heart just about stopped beating when I saw the wreck. I was so relieved when Rafael finally climbed out of his car and walked under his own steam to the ambulance. Is he really okay?"

"He appears to be." Only to herself would Caitlin admit that watching him over the past days move slowly, stiffly, without his usual effortless grace, had driven the point home of how much more serious his injuries could have been. Each time her thoughts wandered that way, she'd relived those terrifying moments she'd spent in the garage, staring at the monitor while praying he hadn't been seriously hurt.

Now, though, wasn't the time to allow her thoughts to drift there. She sipped her coffee before adding, "I haven't had a chance to talk to Rafael much since the race."

Emma-Lee had been right when she'd said Rafael, members of his team and other key individuals would be huddled in meetings after they returned to Charlotte. Caitlin had spent the past two days learning about the city that Rafael had adopted as his new home for inclusion in the profile.

Speaking of the profile, she thought, she'd accepted Emma-Lee's invitation to the Tuesday Tarts meeting in the hopes of learning information about Rafael that didn't have anything to do with racing. It was time she got started.

"So, Rue, do you know Rafael well?"

"Don't I wish? If I were ten years younger, I'd be tempted to go after that fine specimen of a man." Rue's forehead wrinkled. "I hate to admit it, but I haven't even had luck making him a business client."

"Of your beauty shop?"

"Yes, but I don't expect Rafael—or any man—to settle down with the ladies. Not too long ago I remodeled a room and had it set up just for men. I have a lot of male clients now. So far, Rafael isn't one of them."

Rue glanced toward the doorway. "There's my client now."

Caitlin's gaze followed Rue's to the slim woman dressed in a got-to-be designer suit, a navy ribbon belt tied artfully around the waist. Her dark hair, frosted with silver streaks, hung in a sleek, chin-length sweep.

Rue waved the woman over. "Caitlin, this is Doris Martin, my friend and financial adviser. Doris, this is Caitlin Dempsey, a reporter writing a profile on Rafael O'Bryan."

Just then, two more women stepped through the door. Rue excused herself to go greet them.

"Aren't you the lucky one," Doris said while shaking Caitlin's hand.

"Why is that?"

"You have access to Rafael O'Bryan. Like Rue said, I'm a financial adviser. I represent numerous race car drivers, team owners and others involved in racing. I've been trying to book an appointment with O'Bryan for the past year. In fact, he's the *only* NASCAR driver I've yet to even get a chance to talk business with."

"Maybe he uses a different adviser?" Caitlin suggested while the other woman poured a mug of coffee.

"Not according to the financial grapevine around here." Doris blew across the steaming liquid before taking a sip. "Have you seen where he lives?"

"I will tomorrow. I've scheduled a photo shoot at his condo. Why?"

"It's in a nice enough area of town," Doris said. "But considering what a NASCAR driver of O'Bryan's caliber makes each season, he could afford to settle in a much more affluent location. I imagine the inside of the place is as nondescript as the outside. O'Bryan hasn't even treated himself to a flashy sports car, which a lot of drivers do when their earnings increase."

Caitlin knew exactly what he'd earned over his NASCAR career because it was a matter of public record. She had also looked into his past winnings during his go-karting days. The total amount of money was impressive.

Doris took another sip. "It's a mystery to me what the man does with his money."

Caitlin thought about the surgery Rafael had financed for the little girl in Ecuador. "He could make private donations to worthy causes."

"If so, he's doing a good job of keeping them quiet."

"Maybe he spends his money on women," Caitlin tossed out, telling herself it was a supposition any investigative reporter worth her salt would make. "Or one specific woman."

"That would be one lucky female," Doris murmured. "But I doubt that's the case since I've never heard mention of him seeing anyone on a steady basis." As she spoke, Doris flicked a wrist. "It's just a rare thing for someone who participates in such a public sport to avoid the spotlight the way O'Bryan does. It's almost as if the man has gone out of his way to stay offstage and in the shadows. I wonder why."

You're not the only one, Caitlin thought. That same issue had looped through the reporter track of her brain since the day she'd snagged this assignment.

A round of laughter from the other women filled the air. Doris looked at Caitlin. "Guess it's time we join the party."

"I agree." Now more curious than ever about Rafael, Caitlin carried her coffee mug to the nearest empty chair. Since she had yet to see where he lived, the issue of how he spent his income on the long term hadn't come up. Now it was a bright blip on Caitlin's radar.

She glanced at the other women. She'd been to enough races to recognize the wives of several NASCAR drivers. Another was married to the owner of one of the race teams. Before the night was over, Caitlin intended to speak to each of them about Rafael.

Hopefully their input would fill in some of the blanks about the man who guarded information about himself with a secrecy the CIA would envy.

THE FOLLOWING AFTERNOON, Caitlin sat at the small work nook carved out of one corner of Rafael's kitchen, her notepad sharing space with his laptop computer. Pete, the freelance photographer she'd used at National Steel Buildings' health fair, was busy snapping pictures of Rafael deftly chopping ingredients, then tossing them into a pot on the stove.

The kitchen was hunter-green with pristine white woodwork, a ceramic-tile floor and stainless-steel appliances that looked serviceable. As did the furnishings Caitlin had glimpsed when Rafael led her from the front entryway, through the living room and into the kitchen. The condo was clean and tidy, but far from elegant. She studied his laptop while a screensaver sent stock cars speeding across its display. The computer was definitely a few years old.

As Doris Martin had predicted the previous evening, the furnishings and decor inside the condo did nothing to indicate its owner had racked up heart-stopping race winnings.

Which was about all Caitlin had learned at the Tuesday Tarts meeting. None of the other attendees had been able to give her additional insights about Rafael. She'd left Maudie's diner for her hotel room, wondering if there was anyone in the entire world who had the answers to what lay beneath the surface and motivated the man.

She certainly didn't!

Scowling, she gazed at him across the kitchen. Today he'd

paired slacks with a silky-looking turtleneck, both as coal-black as his hair. The bright lights over the stove seemed to enhance his olive complexion. Not to mention those lady-killer eyes that were too blue for his own good.

And hers.

Standing there, a dish towel draped over one shoulder, Mr. Brazil looked so smokin' hot she was tempted to hose herself down.

She bit off a sigh while the glorious scent of simmering sauce wafted over her. *The heartthrob of NASCAR* might be cooking for her, but this was not a social visit. Her editor had insisted on a Rafael-at-home angle in the profile, and with prompting from Gil Sizemore, he had agreed to the provision…grudgingly.

"Need any more shots before I leave for my next assignment?"

Pete's question pulled Caitlin out of her thoughts. After a quick mental review of the pictures he'd taken since he arrived, she shook her head. "I think we've got enough."

He packed his camera in its case, then slung the strap over one shoulder. "I'll get the pics to you sometime tomorrow."

"Fine."

While Pete said goodbye to Rafael, then headed toward the door, Caitlin glanced at the recipe she'd jotted on her notepad.

"So, how often do you cook *feijoada*?"

He grinned, his eyes lingering on her as he used a long-handled wooden spoon to stir the pot. "Your pronunciation is flawless."

"Thank you."

"You're welcome."

Huffing out a breath, she rose, moved to one side of the stove and peered into the pot's bubbling contents. "Are you going to answer my question? Or do you consider your cooking schedule a matter of grave secrecy, like most every other detail of your life?"

Sardonic amusement played around his mouth. "Do you always show so much frustration to the athletes you interview?"

"Just the ones who waffle around answers like a politician on the stump."

"*Feijoada* is the national dish of Brazil, traditionally served on a Saturday. Nine months of the year I spend my weekends at a race track. So, to answer your question as to how often I cook this, or anything, the answer is—seldom."

"Do you ever get tired?"

"Of?"

"Being gone so much. Spending all those weekends on the road."

"It was…difficult at first. I'm used to it now."

She leaned against the counter, watching him stir the pot. "Your fans will appreciate this glimpse of a side of you they don't know."

"Maybe, but my fans are not why I'm cooking today. I've made this dish for you, Caitlin." He laid the wooden spoon aside. "*Feijoada* is considered a festive meal to be shared with close friends."

The fact his accented voice had dropped one octave lower when he'd said *close friends* should not have tightened every muscle in her belly. Yet it did.

"You must try this wine." He retrieved two glasses from a cabinet, then reached for the bottle that had been breathing on the counter. "It, too, is from my native country."

"I didn't realize there was Brazilian wine." Had her voice really gone husky, or was it just her imagination?

"My country is not all rain forests, beaches and the samba," he said while filling the glasses. "The southern area is more temperate and farther from the equator. Italian immigrants settled there in the 1880s and began growing the crop that has turned into a major industry."

She sampled the wine. It was hearty, with a touch of sweetness. "Interesting."

"The wine, or the history about Brazil?"

"Both."

"I agree." He touched his glass to hers before taking a sip.

Caitlin watched him over the rim of her glass. Something like regret, only more complex, flickered briefly in his blue eyes. "Is something wrong?"

"I was thinking that it's been a very long time since I've been there."

"Do you plan to go back?"

"Someday, perhaps." He set his glass aside. "Will you stay and have dinner with me? I know you've come here on business, but I would like to share this special meal with you."

To give herself a moment to think, Caitlin took a long swallow of wine. Just being in close proximity to the man started an alarm blaring in her head. She couldn't deny she wanted to be with him. *Wanted him.* But those type of yearnings were strictly physical and could be controlled.

What she didn't have a handle on was the mix of emotions swirling inside her. She couldn't even identify them, much less control them. But that was the woman in her talking. The investigative reporter was vividly aware this was the first time she and Rafael had been alone together for any length of time. She had only two more weeks to spend on this assignment, and she needed to start making substantial progress. Perhaps here, in the relaxed atmosphere of his home where the scents of glorious spices perfumed the air and wine flowed freely, he might open up about himself.

"All right," she said. "I'll stay for a while. I have to meet Emma-Lee at the mall later."

He nodded. "Sounds like you've made a friend."

"A good one."

After Rafael served the *feijoada*, they ate at the high counter that separated the kitchen from the living room, their long-legged stools only inches apart. During the meal, Caitlin asked him about last Sunday's wreck.

"I'd have been totally terrified," she said after he gave her a detailed account.

"I was too busy trying to keep the car on the track to feel anything," he said, before dishing up another bite.

"Understandable. But after it was over, and you were on your way home, what did you feel?"

"Bruises. Aches and pains."

She shook her head. "I meant emotionally."

"*Gratitude* that I was still around to feel all those bruises, aches and pains."

"Does being in an accident like that make you think twice about climbing into your race car next Sunday?" As she spoke, she slid her half-full plate aside.

"No. For me, racing is equivalent to breathing. It's something I must do." He gestured his wineglass toward her plate. "You didn't like the *feijoada*?"

"I *loved* it. But I'm stuffed." She rested a forearm on the counter. "Who taught you to cook like a pro?"

When he swiveled his stool toward hers, their knees bumped. He adjusted by sliding his thighs on either side of hers. The intimate contact made her nerves shimmer.

"I don't want to talk about myself right now."

"There's some breaking news," she managed to get out past the lump that had formed in her throat.

"I'd rather talk about you."

"Remember the day we met? I told you I'm the interviewer, not the interviewee. That means we talk about you, not me."

"So you did." He set his glass on the counter, then took her hand in his. "Perhaps we should do something other than talk?"

Her body was aware—*very aware*—of his nearness, responding to it in ways that were instinctive and fundamentally feminine—warming, melting. With the counter on one side of her and Rafael on the other, she was caught between an immovable object and an irresistible force.

"If I'm not mistaken," she began, "we agreed to keep things between us on a business level."

"I seem to remember that, too. Although it escapes me now why we thought that was a wise decision."

She looked down at their joined hands. At some point, his long, bronzed fingers had twined with hers. "I'm sure...we had a good reason. At the time."

"I imagine you're right." His thumb stroked the pulse point in her wrist.

She couldn't control the shiver that raced beneath her flesh. The man was going to give her heart failure.

He put a finger under her chin, nudged upward. "So, Caitlin Dempsey, why don't we agree to not talk?"

He was going to kiss her. She knew it; she could read the intention in his eyes, could see the intense longing that matched her own.

She should have moved. She should have stopped him. The events of the past had taught her the bitter consequences of emotional involvement. She had sworn never again to jump into a relationship with a man she didn't know inside and out. Besides, this was business. Rafael was just one more athlete to be added to the long list she'd interviewed and be treated with the same objectivity. He had no business touching her and she had no business wanting him to.

Her heartbeat thrummed with the urgency of an engine

revving on the starting line. She held her breath, waiting, watching, as his mouth drew closer.

She should have stopped him.

But she didn't.

CHAPTER FIVE

WHEN RAFAEL'S LIPS grazed hers, Caitlin didn't protest. She didn't lean away. She wasn't sure she continued to breathe. Not when every emotion she had felt since the instant she'd met him had been honed down to one: desire. Unexplainable. Unbeatable. Unquenchable.

Undeniable.

His fingers were still tangled with hers, warm against her flesh. In an unconscious gesture, she lifted her free hand, placed her palm against his chest. His muscles were rock hard and she could feel his heartbeat, jerking and scrambling in time with hers.

His mouth traveled down the length of her throat, leaving a trail of heat. She let her breath out slowly between her teeth to keep from moaning. It didn't matter whether she trusted him or not, she thought hazily. Didn't matter what she knew about him, what she didn't know, what she thought she knew. All that mattered was that she was here now, with him.

His mouth settled on hers. Gently, this time. Not with the abrupt and shocking flash of heat she'd felt when he kissed her before. This was warm, lazy seduction.

Her lips parted beneath his. He tasted of wine and hot spices, and she melted, slowly, luxuriously, beneath his touch.

What was he doing to her? How could he make her feel so many different things in so short a time?

When his mouth shifted on hers, the kiss tumbled her

deeper, bombarding her with emotions she had no defense against. She could tell herself again and again that she wouldn't fall for this man. That she *couldn't* fall for a man she barely knew. But her heart was already laughing at logic.

Yet, a tiny part of her mind that remained lucid reminded her that giving her heart away hurt.

Still, she wanted him, she thought feverishly. She wanted him, and damn the consequences.

That last thought came so clearly, so simply. And started sharp wings of panic fluttering in her belly.

With an effort, she thrust the heel of her hand against his chest, and felt the corded strength in him as she eased back on her stool. Fighting to catch her breath, she stared at Rafael and saw the hunger that gripped her mirrored in his eyes.

The knowledge his desire matched hers played havoc with her fast-shredding common sense. What kind of power did he have that he could turn her from a sensible, responsible woman into a trembling puddle of need?

"This isn't…" She drew away, let her hand drop from his chest. He kept his fingers linked with hers.

"This isn't, what?" His voice was very quiet, with rough edges.

"What I…should be doing," she managed to say. "I didn't intend to…" She closed her eyes. It was hard to think with desire warring against logic.

"To what? Kiss me?"

"More than that." Her nerves were shimmering now. Sitting so close to him made her feel caught. Defenseless. Out of control. She tugged her hand from his and stood.

A wave of dizziness hit her and she gripped the back of the stool. She wasn't light-headed, she told herself. She'd simply risen too quickly.

"Get involved," she answered. "If I keep kissing you, I'll get involved with you. That's not what I want."

"Why not?" He rose, too, but with an ease that seemed to move muscle by muscle. He reached out for the braid that draped over one of her shoulders, then trailed his fingertips down the knotted cable. "Why don't you want to get involved?"

"Because I don't know you. I don't know who you are."

"Isn't that why people enter into relationships? To get to know each other?"

"That's one reason. Unfortunately, sometimes all they learn is what a huge mistake they'd made by hooking up."

His fingers slid from her braid. "You sound like you're talking from experience."

"I am." She tightened her grip on the back of the stool.

It occurred to her she could be perverse, refuse to explain anything about her past, just as Rafael had done countless times. But she had pulled away from him twice and she wanted him to understand why. *Needed* him to understand.

"My first job out of college was writing obits for my hometown newspaper. When an opening came up covering sports, I talked the editor into giving me a try. About that same time I met a guy named Thane Summers." Caitlin paused. It was hard, even now, to say his name.

"He worked as an on-air reporter for a local station. He was handsome and charismatic and was determined to move up to an anchor job at a cable-news network."

Because her throat had gone dry, Caitlin retrieved her glass off the counter, took a bracing sip of wine. "We'd dated about six months when an armed man started confronting women in the parking lots of various health clubs. He assaulted and robbed them."

She replaced her empty glass on the counter, met Rafael's gaze. The desire she'd seen in his eyes only moments before was gone. Now, his expression was impenetrable.

"Driving race cars is your passion," she continued. "Being

the best damn investigative reporter around is mine. So when the health-club crimes started, I went to my editor, told him I'd hammer at him until he assigned me the story."

"I take it you got your way."

Caitlin nodded. "I lived and breathed that case. Memorized the police reports. I contacted a friend from high school who was a detective. After swearing me to secrecy, he gave me the name of a suspect they'd focused on. But they hadn't questioned him at that point because they didn't have enough evidence to prove anything."

"And if they had talked to him, he'd have taken off," Rafael concluded. He crossed his arms over his chest. "I have a feeling you're going to tell me the suspect's name accidentally got out."

"There was no *accident* to it." Years-old anger and loathing…and, yes, hurt, still gripped her. "Thane had spent the night at my place. When I was in the shower, he stumbled over my case notes and saw the suspect's name. That same day he announced the man's name on the air as 'breaking news.'"

"Which put you in a lot of hot water with the police."

"*Boiling* water. The suspect disappeared—no surprise there. I had to prove to the police, to my editor, that I'd kept my promise not to reveal the suspect's name. So, I wore a wire and confronted Thane. He admitted going through my notes. When I asked why he announced the suspect's name, Thane said it was because he wanted his station to win the ratings for that period. It didn't even faze him that a bad guy was still running around free. All Thane cared about was boosting his own career."

Caitlin clenched her fists against the memories. "I thought I knew him. We'd been lovers for months, and I thought I knew the type of man he was. Turns out, I didn't know him at all."

"Now you look at every man with a jaundiced eye," Rafael said quietly. "Unwilling to give anyone a chance."

Her chin came up. "My 'jaundiced eye' mostly applies to men who expect me to take them at face value. Like you."

"Caitlin." He stepped toward her, but didn't reach out. "There are things I can't reveal to you. People I can't tell you about."

"Can't or won't?"

"Both." He dipped his head, his eyes intense. "People could lose their lives if certain information got out."

"What information? What people?"

"The ones I care about most in the world." He lifted a hand, traced a fingertip along the line of her jaw. "I told you the other night that you've changed things for me. Many things. I have deep feelings for you, Caitlin."

Because his touch had her heart thudding all over again, she took a step back.

Just then, his cell phone rang. He pulled it out of his pocket, glanced at its display. His dark brows pulled together in frustration. "I've been expecting this call for days. It's important. I must take it."

"Go ahead." Legs unsteady, she turned and moved to the work nook where she'd left her notepad beside his computer.

When Rafael answered the call in his native Portuguese, her teeth clenched. Which was a stupid reaction. Instead of thinking he didn't want her to eavesdrop, it could simply be that the caller was a Brazilian friend or acquaintance who didn't speak English. Except that Rafael had claimed he'd lost touch with all friends and acquaintances from his past.

A claim that could be true. Or false. And maybe the caller was one of those people he couldn't tell her about….

Her frustration mounting, Caitlin grabbed the notepad. It jostled the laptop's mouse. The roaring stock-cars screensaver flicked off, replaced by an e-mail that flashed on the monitor.

Wire transfer successful. Shipment confirmed. Delivery next week.
Anne

Caitlin stared at the message. Wire transfer? Shipment? Delivery? *Anne?*

In reporter mode now, her mind instantly read all sorts of hidden meaning behind those words. Both nefarious and innocent.

"Caitlin?"

She glanced over her shoulder. Rafael was off the phone and standing only a few inches away.

"Sorry." She gestured toward the monitor. "I bumped the mouse with my notepad. The screensaver disappeared and this e-mail came up." She turned to face him. "Wire transfer, shipment, delivery," she said lightly. "Did you score something cool on eBay?"

"No." A look crossed his face, a quick shadow, before he leaned past her, touched the mouse and closed the program.

The knots already in Caitlin's shoulders clenched tighter. He claimed she had changed things for him. If that was true, she had no idea what those things were. He had touched her, kissed her, yet he was as uncommunicative as the day they met.

She gave her watch a pointed look. "If I don't leave now, I'll be late meeting Emma-Lee."

Rafael's face looked tense, his eyes cheerless in the kitchen's light. "Will you be on the team plane tomorrow for the flight to California?"

"I plan to be."

Turning, she retrieved her purse, slid her notepad inside.

Her gaze shifted to the monitor where the stock cars had resumed racing. Investigative reporting was all about digging for answers. Relentless inquiry. Focus on details. *The Quest.*

Since Rafael O'Bryan refused to tell her the truth, she would find it herself.

FOR RAFAEL, the following days were an exercise in frustration. It didn't matter that his No. 499 car rolled off the hauler at the California raceway in great shape. Or that he'd had no complaints about the car's performance during practice. Or that he'd qualified for the number-four starting position.

The thing that stayed in the forefront of his mind was his relationship with Caitlin. More like *non*relationship.

It didn't sit well knowing she considered him the equivalent of the half-wit TV reporter who'd betrayed her in favor of ratings week. Rafael kept telling himself he should just shrug it off, forget her and focus on today's race.

Too bad he wasn't having any luck doing that.

It had been four days since the photo shoot at his condo. Since then, he'd seen Caitlin on the team plane where she'd settled into a seat as far from his as possible. She'd kept busy conducting interviews with employees at the raceway and the fans who had shown up to watch the qualifying laps.

It was beyond annoying that he'd made it his business to know where she was and what she was doing. Dammit, she was a reporter, assigned to write a profile. It would show up in *Sports Scene* magazine soon. Then she would move on. And he'd be free of her poking and prodding about things he had one hell of a good reason to keep secret.

In the past, her leaving would have suited him just fine. He'd always been too busy, too focused on his career, too angled in on the next race to take a good, long look at his life. But over the past days, he had found himself doing just that.

And became aware of an emptiness that had been collecting inside him for a long time.

He wanted a life with a woman he loved. Wanted children. A family. A future outside of himself. He wanted to feel needed. Leaned on. He was, for the first time in his adult life, tired of his lone-wolf status.

He thought about how it had felt to have Caitlin at his condo. To prepare a special meal for a woman he cared about and share wine from his homeland. The entire time she was there he had watched her, thinking he might give quite a bit to have her by his side over the years to soften the edges and warm the shadows.

It was odd and a little frightening to admit he'd developed such deep feelings for her in so short a time. But deep they were, and he knew the only chance he had of keeping her in his future was to come clean about his past.

He'd spent hours weighing the pros and cons. Knew that confiding in her could have deadly ramifications. In the end, he had resolved to lay everything on the line and tell her the truth. Then do the best he could to protect the people he loved. Whatever the consequences, he would deal with them.

First, though, he had a race to win.

Dressed in his uniform, his helmet hooked under one arm, he climbed out of the golf cart that had picked him up after an on-air interview. After thanking the driver, he wove his way through a sea of cars, team members, family members and reporters to the pit stall assigned to his team. He was grateful the stalls were chosen by qualifying position, so it didn't take him long to reach the fourth stall.

Caitlin was the first person he spotted there.

Dressed in dark slacks and a long-sleeved T-shirt sporting Double S Racing's logo, she stood beside a red toolbox as big as a car, talking to a couple of over-the-wall guys. Her profile was to him, her long neck looking almost swanlike with her coppery hair pulled into a tight braid.

Watching her, a hungry, possessive tide rose inside Rafael, tightening his stomach and heating his blood. And underneath that, a sense of calm settled around him, assuring him he'd made the right decision.

Because of the noise from the grandstands and the blaring of the track's PA system, he didn't hear her cell phone ring. Just saw her pull it out of her pocket. She answered the call, while moving to the opposite side of the toolbox.

He felt a sudden urge to ask her to meet him after tonight's flight back to Charlotte. To let her know he needed to talk to her about his past.

He took one step in her direction, when Denton Moss closed in. The crew chief was dressed in team colors, the headphones he would use to communicate during the race looped around his neck.

"Rafael, you'd better get a move on or you'll miss the driver introductions. I don't know about you, but I'd rather not start this race at the back of the pack."

Rafael set his jaw against the frustration he was quickly learning to live with. "I'm on my way."

He gave Caitlin one last look before he turned. He would see her later on the plane, get her to agree to go with him to some quiet place in Charlotte where they could talk things out.

"CAN YOU HEAR ME NOW?"

"Barely." Caitlin pressed her cell phone tighter against her ear as she stepped around the big red toolbox in the rear of the pit stall. It was hard to hear Steve Silberg's voice with the race track's PA system blaring and the constant roar of the crowd in the grandstands. At least the race hadn't started.

Trying to hear on the phone with V-8s revving would be next to impossible.

Four days had passed since she told the IT guru at *Sports Scene* magazine about the e-mail Rafael had received. Since then, the language in the message had grabbed onto her brain and wouldn't let go.

Wire transfer successful. Shipment confirmed. Delivery next week.
Anne

Caitlin had spent hours gnawing over the possibility that Rafael was involved in some sort of illegal activity. And the same amount of time assuring herself she was wrong, that the man she cared deeply about was honest. Upstanding. Even so, anxiety knotted her belly at the prospect Steve was about to confirm her worst fears about Rafael.

She pressed her fingers over her free ear to block out the background noise. "Were you able to trace the source of the e-mail just by my giving you those two e-mail addresses?"

"Is a hog's butt pork? Of course I traced it."

Caitlin rolled her eyes. Steve took great exception at the slightest hint he might be unable to perform life-changing miracles when it came to anything computer.

"Don't keep me in suspense," she said. "Where was this Anne chick who wrote the e-mail?"

"At the Nossa Senhora Aparecida in Corumbá, Brazil."

"I've never heard of Corumbá."

"Ditto for me. But since Brazil's almost as big as the lower forty-eight, that's no surprise. I did some quick research and found out Corumbá is in far western Brazil on the Paraguay River, seven miles from the Bolivian border. Which puts a big, nefarious cloud over the e-mail's mention of shipments, payments and delivery."

"Why?"

"Corumbá is one of Brazil's main ports of entry for drugs and arms. They're smuggled over land and via the river."

Caitlin closed her eyes. Her mouth had gone bone-dry and her hands were shaking. Oh, God! Was that what Rafael worked so hard to hide? Was he smuggling drugs? Arms? Nausea churning in her stomach, she wet her lips.

"What exactly is the Nossa Senhora Aparecida?"

"A clinic, named after the patron saint of Brazil. English translation is Our Lady of Aparecida. I'll put the clinic's location and the info I found on Corumbá in an e-mail to you."

"Thanks, Steve," she somehow got out. "Anything else?"

"Just that it's possible you've stumbled onto a big story. If so, your editor's gonna love you."

"Yeah." *The story.* "I have another question."

"About?"

"Your tracking that e-mail. Everything was aboveboard, right?"

"You mean, did I do anything illegal that could prevent your using the info to source your story? The answer is no. I just did a whole lot of creative stuff."

Caitlin ended the call. The only thing that kept her on her wobbly legs was the first notes of the national anthem blaring over the PA system.

Was it within the realm of possibility that Rafael was involved in drug distribution? Gunrunning? Was that the reason he claimed to have no friends in Brazil? Not one connection in that huge country she could contact?

At his condo, he had admitted there were things and people he couldn't tell her about. *People could lose their lives if certain information got out,* he'd said.

Well, no kidding. Gunrunners and dope dealers all shared that common problem.

Despite the suspicious part of her brain alerting her like a drug-sniffing dog on the trail of a suspect, her thoughts went to the little girl in Ecuador whose surgery Rafael had financed. He'd even picked up the tab to fly her extended family there. Could his involvement with the mysterious Anne and Nossa Senhora Aparecida Clinic be on the same Good Samaritan basis?

If that were the case, why could people die if that information got out? And why keep his involvement in such a good cause secret? Why refuse to even admit to *her* that he still had contacts in Brazil? Contacts like Anne.

Caitlin barely heard the escalation in crowd noise as the cars took off. Not when every journalistic fiber of her being screamed to her that Steve was right when he predicted she may have stumbled onto a big story.

One that could enhance her career.

And maybe break her heart.

She curled her fingers into her palms. Before she'd taken on this assignment, she wouldn't have wavered about what her next step should be. She would already be on the phone with her editor.

Instead, here she stood, considering what odds she faced if she confronted Rafael. Demanded he explain what sort of shipments and deliveries he was involved in.

Even her heart knew those odds were far too long to bet on. For the past three weeks Rafael had been like a clam with a broken hinge—she couldn't get anything out of him. She'd be fooling herself to think he would all of a sudden turn talkative.

Squaring her shoulders, she reminded herself that investigative reporting was like SWAT duty. Get in, do your thing, get out. Get too involved in someone's life and—never fails—you get into trouble.

On a low moan, she rubbed at the headache brewing in her forehead. She'd spent the past four days physically distancing herself from Rafael when all she'd wanted was to be near him. *With him.* Now, she was seconds away from calling her editor to get the okay to head to Brazil.

While the thunderous roar of V-8s filled the air, she took a moment to ask herself how she felt about Rafael. Really *felt* about him. She was in deep, she knew that much.

And that was her problem, wasn't it? She'd gotten in over her head with a man before, and he'd betrayed her. Maybe her taste in men hadn't improved and she was afraid that Rafael would do the same.

Caitlin acknowledged it wasn't just the quest for the story that fueled her pressing need to hop the first plane to Brazil and check out what Rafael was involved in. It was because of what had happened between her and her ex-lover.

Never again would she just sit back and wait for answers.

She intended to find them for herself.

CHAPTER SIX

THE FOLLOWING DAY, after spending more than twenty hours on assorted airplanes, Caitlin landed in Corumbá, Brazil. Francisco Ruiz, the professional guide and interpreter hired by *Sports Scene* magazine, met her at the airport.

With the late-afternoon heat shimmering off the hood of Ruiz's dusty car, they drove through the bustling border town surrounded by lush vegetation where commerce and mining thrived.

Although Rafael had lived on the other side of the vast country, in São Paulo, Caitlin tried to imagine what it must have been like for him, growing up in Brazil. Had he and his late parents lived in luxury? Or perhaps in a neighborhood like this one, where merchants sat in the shade of their storefronts, chatting with each other while waiting for customers?

She blew out a breath against the muggy, humid air that made the tendrils that had escaped her braid stick to her clammy skin. Her imaginings about Rafael were a waste of time. He didn't want her to know one iota about how his life had been while growing up. Which was why she was here.

Her attention refocused on the present when Ruiz deftly avoided colliding with a scooter that zipped in front of the car. Most drivers in America—including herself—would have been near the point of violence. Ruiz simply mumbled something in Portuguese that sounded like an oath. Then he shrugged and began describing the widespread poverty that existed in certain areas of Corumbá where the locals were too wary to venture at night.

"The Nossa Senhora Aparecida Clinic is in the heart of one of those areas," he added in thickly accented English. "To ensure your safety, I must have you away from there before dusk."

Caitlin slid the guide/interpreter a sideways look. He was a dark-complected, compact man in his mid-fifties who looked as tough as a chunk of hickory. If *he* had reservations about hanging around the clinic after dark, no way did she want to be there.

"You say the word when we need to clear out. I'll beat you to the car."

"Good."

Inside the clinic's nearly full waiting room, a ceiling fan stirred the hot air. Over a dozen women sat in chairs lining the walls. Several held infants. Most were pregnant.

In one corner, a handful of toddlers played with molded plastic toys on the concrete floor.

During one of her airport layovers, Caitlin had checked her e-mail and found one from Steve Silberg. The magazine's computer whiz had done additional research, and sent the name of the man who owned the go-kart track in São Paulo where Rafael won the first of many races. Steve had also discovered that the Nossa Senhora Aparecida Clinic was run by a nun called Sister Anne, who was also a medical doctor.

Caitlin glanced again at the waiting patients. The women stared back at her with wide, solemn eyes. What were the chances Rafael was in cahoots with a drug-running, arms-dealing nun who provided health care to pregnant women and children? Slim to none.

Even though she had no idea what the e-mail Sister Anne sent to Rafael meant, the deep-seated instinct Caitlin had developed after years on the job told her there was nothing nefarious going on at this clinic.

Still, that instinct had failed her once when a man she cared about was involved, and she wanted—*needed*—proof.

She stepped to the receptionist sitting behind a scarred desk. When the young woman looked up, light flashed off the lenses of her glasses.

Caitlin handed the woman her business card while introducing herself. Ruiz repeated her words in Portuguese.

"I would like to speak to Sister Anne," Caitlin added.

After Ruiz interpreted the request, the woman answered.

"The sister is with a patient," he relayed. "She has many more waiting to see."

"Ask her to tell Sister Anne I'll wait as long as necessary to speak to her."

After hearing that, the young woman shoved up her glasses, rose and hurried down the corridor behind her desk.

Ruiz glanced at the waiting patients. "We could be here a long time."

"As long as necessary," Caitlin repeated. Then added, "Or until dusk, whichever comes first."

Ruiz nodded, apparently satisfied.

When the receptionist returned, she motioned them to follow her down the same hallway. They passed several closed doors, winding up in a room at the rear of the clinic that contained chairs and a TV-VCR setup. Caitlin theorized the area was used for instructional videos for the patients. On the far side of the room, workmen were in the process of prying off the top of a large wooden crate.

A tall, swarthy workman holding a crowbar lifted a hand in greeting to Ruiz. He nodded.

"A friend of yours?" Caitlin asked.

"Of my cousin's."

Caitlin watched the workmen as they jimmied off enough

wooden slats to reveal something swaddled in cloudy plastic. Since she and Ruiz had been escorted to the room, she had no expectation that this "shipment" contained either illegal arms or drugs. Still, she was curious.

"Can we ask your cousin's friend what's under the plastic?"

Ruiz nodded, then headed across the room. Caitlin trailed behind him, veering toward the lid of the crate that was now propped against one wall. She noted the name of a well-known American company and address on the shipping label.

"According to my cousin's friend, the crate contains a new X-ray machine," Ruiz said when he rejoined her. "A donor in America purchases equipment and medical supplies for the clinic several times a year. This is one of those purchases."

"Thank you," Caitlin said. Deep down she knew that donor was Rafael, and that he spent the majority of his income to help the clinic. Still, she held back the stirrings of relief that should accompany that knowledge. She didn't yet know why he kept those donations secret. Or whose life would be in danger if word of his philanthropy got out.

The sound of footsteps had Caitlin turning.

The woman approaching wore a lab coat over a white blouse and black slacks. She was dark haired, short and thin, somewhere in her thirties. She held Caitlin's business card in one hand.

"Miss Dempsey, I'm Sister Anne." Her voice was as smooth as silk, with no accent.

Caitlin introduced Ruiz, then said, "Thank you for seeing me, Sister. If you could spare some time, I'd like to ask you a few questions."

Sister Anne glanced at the business card. "Perhaps you could first explain what interest a sports reporter has in the Nossa Senhora Aparecida Clinic."

"Actually, my reason for being here is to interview you

about your relationship with Rafael O'Bryan. I understand he's an acquaintance of yours."

Caitlin had hoped the mention of Rafael's name would elicit a reaction from the nun. As it was, she might as well have been sitting at a poker table for all she could tell from Sister Anne's expression.

"Rafael is a dear friend." Sister Anne slid the card into the pocket of her lab coat. "Have you come all the way from America to ask me about Rafael?"

"Yes. I'm writing a profile on Rafael that encompasses more than just his profession. The profile is intended to give his fans insight into his personal life."

The nun's gaze slid down to take in Caitlin's rumpled blouse and slacks. "When did you arrive in Corumbá?"

"About an hour ago."

The combined banging of a hammer and whine of a drill nearly drowned out Caitlin's words.

Sister Anne glanced toward the workmen. "I'm sure you're tired from your long journey," she said, looking back at Caitlin. "Let's talk in my office."

"Thank you."

Since Sister Anne spoke flawless English, Ruiz opted to remain in the room where he could watch the workmen's progress.

In the nun's small office, late-afternoon sun slanted through half-open blinds, casting neat lines across the tidy wooden desk. Overhead, a ceiling fan identical to the one in the waiting room made lazy circles. Sister Anne gestured toward a wooden chair in front of the desk, then made a quick phone call.

Only minutes after Caitlin settled in the chair, the young receptionist arrived, balancing a tray holding two tiny white china cups on saucers.

"Have you had a chance to try *cafezinho?*" Sister Anne asked.

"No." Caitlin accepted the cup and saucer from the receptionist. They reminded her of the set of miniature china that she and her sisters played tea party with while growing up.

"I hope you enjoy it," Sister Anne said. "Like most Brazilians, I'm addicted to it."

Pinching the cup's handle between her thumb and finger, Caitlin took a sip. The black-as-ink coffee was hot and potent and had enough sugar in it to sweeten a birthday cake. After a second sip, she felt a welcome kick to her system.

"It's wonderful."

Nodding, Sister Anne sat back in her chair. "It has been a while since I've spoken to Rafael. He is well?"

"Yes." Caitlin pulled her notepad out of her purse. "How long have you known him?"

"Since we were children."

"Did you go to school together?"

"Yes."

"What school?"

Sister Anne regarded Caitlin over the rim of her cup. "Did Rafael recommend that you come to see me?"

"No."

"He doesn't know you're here, does he?"

"When I write a profile on a sports figure, I don't tell him or her which of their acquaintances I plan to interview. That's not how my job works."

"I imagine you've discovered that Rafael is a very private man. If he wanted you, or his fans, to learn certain information about himself, he would let it be known on his own."

"I understand that, Sister. But his sponsor isn't happy that the fans know so little about Rafael outside of racing. That's why they approached my magazine and suggested the profile. Since we'd be getting full access to Rafael, we decided to pursue the profile. He's one of the most talented drivers in the NASCAR Sprint Cup Series. Because of that, numerous articles have been written about Rafael's involvement in the sport. To be frank, that's old news. The profile I'm writing is focused on who the man is. What happened in his past to bring him where he is today. It's people like you, a childhood friend, who can reveal information about a time in his life that few people know about."

Sister Anne replaced her cup on its saucer. "I can tell you that Rafael is a kind man. Good-hearted. Generous. Protective of those who matter to him. But as to other information about him, that is up to Rafael to reveal."

"Can you tell me if he donates money to your clinic?"

"Policy forbids me to discuss our donors."

Caitlin could feel each individual pulse point in her body throb in frustration. She had purposely shown up here without giving Sister Anne notice so the nun wouldn't have a chance to call Rafael and find out what to, and what not, to say. Even so, the woman had hedging down to a science.

"Sister Anne, I saw an e-mail you sent to Rafael. You mentioned a wire transfer, shipment and delivery. Was that e-mail about the X-ray machine being uncrated in the other room?"

"Rafael showed you that e-mail?"

"In a roundabout way." Caitlin leaned forward. "Did he purchase the X-ray machine for the clinic? Does he regularly donate equipment and medical supplies? Is that what the wire transfers, shipments and deliveries are all about?"

"Again, policy won't allow me to answer." The nun glanced at her watch and rose. "You'll have to excuse me, Miss Dempsey. I have a waiting room full of patients I must see."

Caitlin stayed in her chair. "Why is it a matter of life or death that Rafael keep certain activities he's involved in secret?"

This time, the woman's dark eyes widened. "He told you that?"

"Yes. He said he wouldn't, *couldn't,* explain why. Just that lives were at stake. Is it your life that's in danger, Sister Anne? Or Rafael's? Or both?"

The nun stepped slowly around the desk, pausing a few inches from Caitlin's chair. "Rafael has trusted you with information that, to my knowledge, he has never told another woman. For him to do that tells me there's more to your relationship than just a reporter interviewing an athlete. He must care deeply for you."

Caitlin's heart clenched. She wished she could believe that. "If that were true, he would tell me what's going on."

"Sometimes confiding certain information in a person puts a terrible burden on that individual. An *unnecessary* burden of worry because that person can do nothing about the problem."

"What exactly is the problem, Sister?"

"It is Rafael's place to tell you." Reaching out, the nun placed a hand gently on Caitlin's shoulder. "You care for him, too. I can see it in your eyes."

Feeling far too uncomfortable under the woman's discerning gaze, Caitlin rose. "Thank you for your time, Sister," she said, hating that the raw emotion churning inside her had settled in her voice.

Over the past days, she hadn't allowed herself to examine her feelings for Rafael. Hadn't wanted to delve into how deeply those feelings had grown in such a short time. What would be the point? After all, she fully expected Sister Anne to call Rafael and let him know she'd shown up, asking about his and the nun's relationship.

A man as fanatically private as Rafael O'Bryan would view her actions as the equivalent of a betrayal.

And that, Caitlin thought, would be the end of things.

Rafael spotted Caitlin the instant she wheeled her suitcase into the lobby of the Charlotte hotel. Glancing at his watch, he noted it was a few minutes past midnight. He remained seated in the chair he'd chosen in the out-of-the-way corner. He'd been there, waiting, for the past hour.

After Sister Anne called to clue him in about Caitlin's visit, he had made it his business to find out the exact time she boarded a plane in Corumbá. Upon arriving in São Paulo, she had taken a cab to the go-kart track that had served not only as his workplace, but his home. He knew exactly how long she spent there before heading back to the airport to catch a flight to the States. She'd had a three-hour layover in Atlanta before leaving for Charlotte.

Now, she was back.

In his sights.

His narrowed gaze skimmed up her, from the slim jeans that made her legs look long and coltish to the dark green blouse that reached to midthigh and was cinched with a leather belt. Her hair was loose, the rich, wild tumble of fiery auburn streaming over her shoulders.

Despite the anger brewing inside him, he remembered how it felt to slide his fingers through those long tendrils that clung to his hands like licks of a flame. The memory had heat coiling in his gut, a great gnawing ache. For a few seconds, he couldn't shove back the memory of how it felt to hold her. Kiss her.

With a silent curse, he rose. He hadn't come here to do either. He intended to talk. To let her know exactly how he felt about her forcing herself on the two people who meant most to him in the world. People who now might be in even more danger because of her.

He'd gotten Caitlin's room number from Emma-Lee, so he held back, watching as she waited for an elevator. She rubbed a palm over the back of her neck, a gesture of such weariness that he struggled against a feeling of empathy.

Fisting his hands, he watched her step onto the elevator, followed by an elegantly dressed man and woman. When the elevator doors slid closed, he headed for the staircase. What he had to say to her, he would say in private.

In her room.

Alone.

WITH FATIGUE ROLLING over her like fog, Caitlin slid her key card into the lock on the door of her hotel room. All she wanted was to crawl into bed and sleep for about five years.

In the next instant, a hand settled on her wrist. She jolted. Then swallowed the shriek welling up her throat when she saw who the hand belonged to.

"Rafael."

"Welcome back."

In the brightly lit hallway, he looked anything but welcoming with his mouth set in a grim line and his eyes resembling hard, blue ice.

Since his fingers were still wrapped around her wrist, it was a sure bet he felt her pulse jittering. "I planned on coming to see you tomorrow," she said.

"Plans change." He grabbed the handle of her suitcase. "I came to see you instead."

"So you did." Her stomach tight with nerves, it took her two attempts to get the key card into the lock. She watched as he rolled the suitcase into the room. The door closed behind him with a metallic snap.

After dropping her purse on the bed, she turned to face him. "I imagine you got a call from Sister Anne."

"And from Érico Braga after you left the go-kart track in São Paulo. Why did you go to Brazil, Caitlin?"

"Why do you think? You've spent the past three weeks

telling me next to nothing about your past. Your mistake was expecting me to just accept that. I don't take anything at face value."

"Because you got burned once."

"It was a learning experience. My career took a huge hit. I don't intend for that to happen again."

"It's a shame you can't trust."

"The same goes for you, Rafael. I base my stories on facts. *Corroborated* facts. You refused to give me anything to work with, so I went to Brazil. Period."

"Did you find out all you need to know about me?"

She matched his steely gaze. "You know I didn't. It's obvious Sister Anne and Érico Braga care deeply about you. And know you well. But all either would tell me about you were generalities. I hope you appreciate their loyalty."

"I do."

Because her feet were killing her, she kicked off her shoes. "Do you know what was going on at the go-kart track when I got there?"

"Why don't you tell me?"

"More kids than I could count were riding the karts, having a blast. Érico Braga explained that one afternoon a week, he opens the track for children whose families are too poor to pay to rent the go-karts." She stepped toward Rafael. "But you already know that, don't you? Because I'll bet my only pair of Italian stilettos that you fund those sessions."

When he didn't answer, she shook her head. "You don't need to worry, because Érico Braga wouldn't confirm that, either. Nor would Sister Anne verify that *you* purchased the X-ray machine I saw being uncrated. Or that you pay for the shipments of equipment and medical supplies that arrive at the clinic from an anonymous donor several times a year. Even so, I suspect you're their personal philanthropist. Instead of living in the lap of luxury here, you donate a great deal of your NASCAR winnings to worthy causes there."

"You have no proof of that."

"Doesn't matter. I've been an investigative reporter long enough to know when I should listen to what my gut's telling me. In this case, it's sending the message that I'm right."

Her frustration growing, she curled her fingers into her palms. "In my line of work, I expect people to lie to me. The reasons vary—self-preservation, embarrassment, a need to gloss over the image. It's up to me to find the reasons for the lie."

"I haven't lied to you, Caitlin."

"Well, you've done a spiffy job of erecting roadblocks when it comes to me finding out the truth about anything that doesn't directly apply to your racing career. My problem is, I can't figure out why. What's your motivation? Why keep the good stuff you do secret, when publicizing it would be a plus for everyone? It's exactly the type of PR your sponsor wants people to know. Your fans would eat it up. Tons of them would send donations to Sister Anne's clinic. There's no downside."

"There is," he countered, his eyes darkening to the hue of a stormy sea. "I told you that people could lose their lives if certain information about me got out. You think that's not a downside?"

"I don't know what to think because you're not willing to explain anything. You just expect me to accept it as the truth."

"Damn right." He took a step toward her. "Every situation is different. I'm not some athlete who decides he doesn't like media interviews, so he gives you a bad time. I have a good reason for keeping certain information to myself without having to explain why."

Biting back a soft shriek of frustration, she pivoted, stalked to the far side of the room. Dragging in a few deep breaths, she counted to ten. Then counted again before turning.

"One of the basic things I learned in Journalism 101, is that you're only as good as your last story. I imagine there's something equal to that in NASCAR racing. It's how you did in your latest race that people talk about. Right?"

"Your point?"

"Suppose I came to you and told you it was a matter of life or death that you place last in the race next weekend in New Hampshire. *Dead last.* But instead of explaining why, I insist you simply take my word for it. That certain unnamed people could be at risk if you don't, and *their* safety is way more important than the career you've worked your butt off to build." She angled her chin. "What would O Tubarão do in that circumstance? Take my word for things? Purposely blow a race just because I asked him to? Hardly."

She knew she'd made her point when Rafael blew out a breath. He rolled his shoulders as if trying to loosen muscles that had knotted there. "No," he agreed tightly. "I would need an explanation."

Caitlin felt a rush of satisfaction, but said nothing as she watched him move to the room's lone window. He hooked a finger at the edge of the curtain, drew it back, then gazed out into the dark night.

"You saw the e-mail Anne sent me," he said, keeping his eyes on whatever was beyond the window. "How did that lead you to her?"

"I memorized her e-mail address. I gave it, and your e-mail addy, to the computer whiz at the magazine. I don't know how, but he tracked the e-mail to the Nossa Senhora Aparecida Clinic."

"So easy," Rafael scoffed. "I've gone to great lengths to ensure my ties to Anne remain hidden. Yet, you found her with little effort."

"I wouldn't have, if not for the computer guy."

Rafael turned from the window, crossed his arms over his chest. There was a hardness in his face that stretched the skin over his high, exotic cheekbones. "My parents died in an accident when I was barely two years old. I have no memory of either of them. Since I had no blood kin, I wound up in an orphanage in São Paulo."

It took Caitlin's jet-lagged brain a few seconds to realize he was actually talking about his childhood. The emotion flooding through her started her hands shaking.

Wordlessly, she lowered onto one corner of the bed and waited for Rafael to continue.

"Then a flu epidemic swept through the town where Anne lived. Her few remaining relatives were too poor to take in another child. She wound up at the same orphanage. For some reason we bonded the first day she arrived. Became fast friends. Basically inseparable."

"How long were you together there?"

"Ten years," he answered. "The buildings were old and poorly maintained. One night, an electrical fire started in the attic of the dormitory where Anne lived. Only half of the kids in that building got out alive." A shadow of old pain flashed in Rafael's eyes. "At first, I couldn't find her. I panicked, tried to run into the burning building. A fireman stopped me."

"But she *had* gotten out," Caitlin said quietly. A hollow feeling inside her belly told her his story was only going to get worse from here.

"Thankfully. I found her with some other kids who'd crawled out through a rear window."

As if trying to shove the memory from his mind, Rafael raked a hand through his dark hair. "It was windy, the fire spread, turning all the buildings on the grounds into a tinderbox. By dawn, everything was gone. The head of the orphanage put out a plea for people to adopt the children who'd survived the fire. Or at least take them in on a foster basis. Anne got lucky—a good, solid family with two daughters took her in."

Caitlin swallowed, feeling pressure build in her throat. "What happened to you?"

"A man and woman showed up. Said they lived in a town on the Bolivian border, that they already had six foster sons, but they could make room for one more. So many children needed homes that background checks on the people who offered to take them weren't done. I was sent home with that couple."

"From your tone, I'm guessing you didn't wind up in a family like the one that adopted Anne."

"Not even close," he answered, his tone derisive. "I didn't know that at first, though. I had never been inside a house that was so big. Elegant. I was thirteen, and I thought I'd wound up in heaven. It turned out to be hell."

"What happened?"

His gaze went past her, and he stood in silence, as if gearing up to tell her what was at the heart of the matter. What he'd said was bad enough, and Caitlin felt a prick of apprehension over whatever had happened in the house that had been a form of hell.

"I hadn't even been there twenty-four hours when one of the older boys named Cruz shoved me against a wall," Rafael said finally. "He referred to my foster father as O Diabo— the Devil. Cruz said I was now O Diabo's property. So were all the police and politicians in town. Then he told me I was a replacement for a boy who'd just died and that I'd better cooperate. If I made a fuss, I'd die, too."

A sick feeling settled in Caitlin's stomach. "What about your foster mother?"

"I never saw her again after we drove to the house." Rafael raised a shoulder. "After Cruz walked off, I tried to sneak out. That's when I found out all the windows had bars and the doors were secured with dead bolts that could only be unlocked with a key."

"So, you were a prisoner." The jittering in Caitlin's stomach echoed in her voice.

"Yes. I found a ventilation vent big enough to get through but the cover was stuck. Then O Diabo yelled for me. When I faced him, I saw a hovering cruelty in his eyes that hadn't been there before. He shoved me into a room that had a table stacked with balloons that were mostly deflated. He picked up a balloon that I could tell had something in it, grabbed me by the back of the neck and told me to swallow the balloon."

"It had drugs inside it, right?"

"Cocaine, to be exact. He told me I had to swallow six balloons. Then I'd be driven to the border. After I crossed into Bolivia, someone would pick me up. He said if I didn't do exactly as I was told, I'd be killed. I was scared to death."

"What did you do?"

"Fought. I knew I might die, but that was preferable to choking down even one of those balloons." His voice edged with old pain, Rafael reached up, rubbed at a spot on his chest. "He pulled a knife out of his boot and slashed me. That's the scar you saw at Maudie's diner when little Lily Donovan pulled my shirt collar open."

Caitlin thought of how close that scar was to his heart, and felt a shudder go through her.

"My wound was more long than deep. Fortunately, the blood made my skin slick. O Diabo couldn't keep a grip on me, or his knife. When he dropped it, I grabbed it and stabbed him. I snatched up a handful of balloons on my dash out the door so that none of the other boys would have to choke them down."

"Did you kill him?"

"I hoped so. Later I learned he'd survived."

"Did you get out of the house through the vent?"

Rafael nodded sharply. "With all the adrenaline pumping through my system, I ripped the cover off with my bare hands. After I got away, I tossed the balloons with the drugs down a sewer."

"What did you do then?"

"Left town. I knew if O Diabo survived, he would try to hunt me down. I changed my name and appearance, made my way back to São Paulo. I soon learned that O Diabo was alive, and that he controlled most of the drug trade there, too. And that he'd put out a contract on a teenager named Marcos Sousa."

"Is that your real name?"

"Yes. I lived on the streets, avoided the drug dealers and made enough money to survive by hawking souvenirs. I also became very adept at picking pockets. I knew the name of the family that adopted Anne, so I went to see her on the sly. After I told her what happened, she wanted to beg her new family to take me in, too, but I wouldn't let her. O Diabo wanted to kill me. It made sense that he would do the same to anyone associated with me. I couldn't put Anne or her family at risk."

"Where did Érico Braga come in?"

"I tried to pick his pocket and he caught me. He's the only person who ever did." For an instant, Rafael's expression softened, then closed off again. "He clamped his hand around my wrist and said it was up to me what happened next. My first choice was to go to jail for attempted larceny."

"What other choice did he give you?"

"Take a job at the go-kart track he owned. I could bunk there and work off the amount of money he had in his pocket. I needed to stay off the radar of all the police, so I took the job. After my first up-close look at the karts, I was hooked."

"Mr. Braga told me the first time you climbed behind the

wheel of a go-kart, he knew you were a natural. That he'd never seen anyone with such an uncanny instinct for forming a winning strategy on a race track." Caitlin couldn't help but smile at the memory of the pride that had glittered in the short, stocky man's eyes when he spoke of Rafael. Suddenly, she realized that bust-button pride had uncoiled the last nagging tendril of doubt she'd harbored about Rafael.

"He's very fond of you," she managed to say.

"He is like a father to me. Anne is in all respects my sister," he added fiercely, protectively. "And O Diabo is now the most powerful drug dealer in Brazil. If he were to learn my true identity and somehow unearth my connections to them, their lives would be worthless. So, out of necessity, I keep a low profile."

"While quietly funneling money to them."

"Yes." He walked to the bed, looked down at Caitlin. She watched a muscle bunch underneath the olive skin of his jaw while the scent of his indescribably male aftershave made her belly go tight.

"I'd already decided to tell you about my past on the night of the California race," he said. "I planned to ask you after we boarded the team plane if you would meet me when we got back to Charlotte. Go somewhere private where we could talk." He shrugged. "But you weren't on the plane. I asked Emma-Lee why. She said she'd gotten a text message from you that said your editor had sent you on assignment, but you hadn't said where."

Caitlin's weary brain honed in on only one thing. "What made you decide to suddenly tell me about your past?"

"I meant it when I told you that you changed things. I didn't accept that at first because so little time has passed since we met. I fought the feelings, refused to acknowledge them. But you'd somehow gotten inside me and what I feel for you has a long reach and a hard grip."

Emotion thudded into her chest, flooded into her heart. "Rafael, I…"

The rest of the words slid back down her throat when he held up a hand. "Let me finish."

She nodded, unable to speak.

"You made me start thinking about the future, Caitlin. How I was pretty sure I wanted you in it. And that I couldn't ask you to be a part of my life when you didn't know the truth about my past."

His words kicked her already racing pulse into high gear. It was then that she realized what she had refused to admit until now. What she had insisted was only a chemical reaction when he kissed her. She was teetering on the edge of falling in love. *So close.* Not just because of his woman-killer sexy accent or the hot-blooded kisses that heated her flesh. But for the man beneath. The man who had fashioned his professional life around protecting the people he loved. The man who freely gave so much of his earnings to help a doctor in a faraway clinic save lives and to provide kids free rides on go-karts.

The man who had opened his past to her so they might share a future.

Her head was spinning. She needed time to think. To adjust. "I…don't know what to say."

"Don't say anything." His eyes were unreadable, his face as hard as carved stone. "You wanted the whole story. You got it. Now you have to decide what to do with it. With *us*."

CHAPTER SEVEN

"How does it feel to win at the New Hampshire track?"

"Great!" Standing in Victory Lane, Rafael grinned his answer into the microphones aimed his way by various reporters. "I never get tired of winning," he added before scrubbing his hands with the towel someone had given him after he'd done the obligatory shaking of a magnum of champagne, then spewing its contents across his celebrating team members.

"Can we get a few more pictures of you with the trophy?"

He had to strain to hear the question over the blare of the PA system and cheers from thousands of race fans in the grandstands. Then there were the hoots and hollers from his champagne-dowsed team members, who were still grinning like fools and giving each other high fives.

"Happy to oblige." Even as Rafael hoisted the trophy, his thoughts weren't totally on the race he'd just won in a breath-stopping finish. They also focused on Caitlin.

He hadn't seen or heard from her since the night he left her hotel room, and he had no expectation she would suddenly appear. Even so, that hadn't stopped him from trying to spot her in the grandstands during his prerace ride around the track in the back of a flag-draped pickup.

There'd been no sign of her in the garage or the pit area, either. Which pretty much told him she had decided to use all the dark, miserable details about his past in the magazine profile.

The repercussions that sole act would have on him and the lives of the two people closest to him had the anger that had brewed inside him for days resurfacing. And with that, the hurt. Dammit, before Caitlin he hadn't let any woman get close, and he hadn't had a problem. With her he'd lowered the walls and let his guard down.

And allowed himself to get close to falling in love with a woman who had the means to blow his world apart.

He went still when he realized where his thoughts had veered. No, he countered, he *cared* for her. A lot. Otherwise he never would have confided in her. Caring was a long, *safe,* distance from the close-to-falling-in-love category. A person could move on from caring for another. He wasn't sure the same applied to loving someone.

"Rafael, how about raising the trophy a little higher?" one of the reporters shouted.

He obliged, keeping his smile in place. Inwardly, he resolved to somehow deal with the aftereffects of Caitlin Dempsey walking into his life…and out of it.

THE SUN-DAPPLED AFTERNOON had slid into early evening by the time Rafael wrapped up his final interview and signed his last autograph for a fan. He grabbed one of the team's golf carts and wended his way back to the motor-home lot, nodding to a few acquaintances he passed.

Normally after a race he'd be in a hurry to change out of his uniform, then head for the airport. Not today. National Steel Buildings had scheduled a reception this evening for some of its franchisees in the area, and he was slated to attend.

Steering toward his motor home, he narrowed his eyes when he spotted someone sitting on the front steps. When he got close enough to confirm it was Caitlin, his chest went tight.

She was dressed in tan slacks and a cream-colored short-sleeved blouse, her auburn hair plaited into a loose French braid. The long rays of the sun lent her skin a healthy glow.

Something much too akin to nerves moved into his stomach.

She stood as he climbed out of the golf cart. Her purse hung from a chain looped over her right shoulder. A manila envelope dangled from one of her hands.

As her gaze met his, he felt the sparks that had kindled between them from the moment they'd met. The memory of their kisses stirred his blood. And a mix of emotion he in no way wanted to acknowledge rolled through him.

THE INSTANT SHE SPOTTED Rafael driving up in the golf cart, Caitlin's mouth went dry. Over the past days she'd ridden an emotional roller coaster that had her questioning her abilities as a reporter, not to mention her saneness as a woman who'd once sworn to protect her scarred heart at all costs.

The realizations she'd finally come to both professionally and personally since she'd last seen Rafael had left her feeling a little dazed.

"Hi," she said, forcing her voice to remain level. "Emma-Lee said you've got a sponsor appearance here tonight. I thought this might be a good place to catch up with you."

He gave her a curt nod. "Haven't seen you around in a while."

"I've been holed up in my hotel room in Charlotte, then the one here. Working." Her nervous fingers tapped against the manila envelope. She should just jump in and tell him it contained the profile. Explain her reasons for why she'd written it as she had. In truth, she knew no matter what she said today, she might have already blown any chance of his wanting to see her again. That thought shot a little arrow of panic straight to her heart.

To give her system time to settle, she said, "Congratulations on today's win."

"Thanks." He still wore his racing uniform that enhanced his wide shoulders and narrow waist. Rays from the setting sun reflected against his mirrored sunglasses as he shifted to rest a foot on the bottom step. "Did you catch the race, or just hear about the results?"

"Emma-Lee and I watched the whole thing from your sponsor's suite." Caitlin glanced in the direction of the suites that towered over parts of the grandstands. "It's quite a different view up there from what you get in the pits."

"Any comments on the race?"

She looked back at Rafael, pursing her lips in thought. "The way you passed the lead car on that restart after the fourth caution was a super-slick maneuver," she said after a moment. "And it was a wise decision during those final laps to just cruise on what fuel you had instead of pitting."

He raised a coal-black brow. "Sounds like you've learned a lot about NASCAR racing."

"I had a good teacher." She tilted her head to study him, but the dark sunglasses prevented her from reading what was in his eyes. "Are you going to invite me in?"

"Is this visit business or pleasure?"

Squaring her shoulders, she held up the envelope. "I brought you an advance copy of the profile. It'll be in *Sports Scene* magazine's next issue. Other than my editor, you'll be the first to read it."

Without comment, he stepped up the stairs, unlocked the door. He moved aside to allow her to enter first.

She caught a whiff of the rich scent of leather before she was fully inside and spotted the dark tufted sofa and matching chairs in the spacious living room. A thick area rug pooled beneath her feet. She shifted her gaze to the kitchen that seemingly had every gadget money could buy, top-of-the-line stainless-steel appliances and granite counters.

He turned to face her. "Before that supersonic inquisitive reporter's mind of yours starts wondering if *this* is actually where my money goes, don't waste the effort. The motor home and all furnishings belong to my sponsor. It's available to me as long as I drive for NSB."

"Before, I might have wondered if this all belonged to you. But not now."

He pulled off his sunglasses, tossed them on the nearby counter that separated the kitchen from the living room. "Why not now?"

"Because I know without a doubt your personal comfort is not what's important to you." Easing out a breath, she laid her purse and the envelope on one end of the leather couch. "Rafael, I didn't come here just to deliver your copy of the profile. There are some things I want to tell you in person. *Need* to tell you."

Keeping his gaze locked with hers, he leaned against the counter. "I'm listening."

"The first draft of the profile I wrote included the information about your early life. The orphanage, the fire, your narrow escape from the drug lord, O Diabo. It was all in there."

She thrust her hands into her pockets, pulled them out again. "After I wrote the draft, I turned off my computer, climbed into bed and tried to shut off my mind. But something hollow had settled inside me and I couldn't sleep. Every journalistic fiber of my being screamed that I was right to include all the facts about your past in the profile. That your telling me the truth had basically given me permission to use the information. That's what any reporter worth her salt would do. Use it."

"So, did you?"

She shook her head, thinking of the long and restless nights behind her. And the lonely ones she might be facing. "No matter what spin I tried to put on it, I always came back to the fact that it wouldn't be *right* to publish that information. Or fair."

He scrubbed a hand over his jaw. "I can't say I'm sorry to hear that."

She moved toward him. "I kept telling myself that it was just a fluke I saw Sister Anne's e-mail to you. I hadn't purposely dug through your files to find out information the way my ex-lover had done. Even so, I realized if I revealed your past it would be no different than his broadcasting a suspect's name on the air. His doing that put innocent people at risk. The same would go for me. You, Sister Anne and Érico Braga are good, honest people. Selfless. You do wonderful things for others. The three of you make a huge difference. I wouldn't be able to sleep nights knowing that I sacrificed your safety and put Sister Anne and Érico Braga in danger all for a story."

"So, how did you make the profile acceptable to your editor?"

"The magazine wanted me to show your fans what kind of person you are. I told my editor I found nothing in Brazil, but I already had enough to make everyone happy. One example of that is what you did for Hector Jonas's baby niece in Ecuador. Paying for her open-heart surgery, then flying Hector, his wife and children there to be with the family will give your fans a new insight into you. Another example is what the crew chief on the first team you drove for when you arrived in the States told me when I interviewed him."

"Which was?"

"You treated his son's grade-school class to a Saturday at a local go-kart track. You didn't just foot the bill—you spent hours there, giving each kid personal instruction on his or her driving." As she spoke, Caitlin flicked a wrist. "Your fans—and your sponsor—are also going to love the part of the profile that gives them an inside look at you while at home and seeing Chef Rafael cooking, serving wine."

Studying her, Rafael angled his head. "You don't exactly sound happy about the decision you made to keep the truth about my past buried."

"It was illuminating, let's put it that way," she replied as she paced in front of him. "I'm an *investigative* reporter, I'm not supposed to let personal feelings interfere with the stories I write. But that's exactly what I did."

Reaching out, he snagged her arm, forcing her to stand still. "Exactly what personal feelings are you talking about?"

"Ones that I still have a hard time believing are there." She closed her eyes, shook her head. "When we first met, you were so shut off. Distant. If I'd never seen the kindness beneath that tough exterior of yours, I could have resisted you. But I did see it."

His killer blue eyes narrowed on her face. "Are you saying you can't resist me?"

"That seems to be one of my major problems."

"What's another?"

"Only the fact that you've had me off balance since we collided in the doorway at Double S Racing. I'm not sure I'll ever find my footing with you." She pulled her bottom lip between her teeth. "There's something else I'm not sure of."

"What?"

"That how I feel about you matters now."

"Why?"

"You said I changed things. Made you start thinking about a future with me in it." She lifted her shoulders. "Things were tense the other night at the hotel when I got back from Brazil. I have no idea what you're feeling now. About us. Me."

"I thought I knew," he said, his expression intense. "Thought I had everything figured out. Then I drove up a few minutes ago and saw you sitting on the front steps."

He looked past her shoulder and fell silent, as if he was gathering his thoughts.

Anticipation had Caitlin's pulse thudding hard and thick at the base of her throat. "And?" she prodded after a moment.

He looked back at her, his eyes somber. "Seeing you, sitting there, waiting on me, it hit me how empty I'd felt over the past days with you gone."

His words started her hands trembling. "I missed you, too, Rafael."

Reaching out, he stroked her cheekbone with his thumb, his expression pensive. "I want you in my life, Caitlin Dempsey. That hasn't changed."

Her lips parted. Her heart began to beat in a quick, almost painful rhythm she recognized as joy. "You mean your crazy life where you're on the road nine months out of the year?" Incredibly moved, she laid her palms on his chest. She felt his rock-hard muscles and beyond them, the steady beating of his heart. "This life where you have to go on dates during the week because your Saturday nights are usually spent at a race track? The life where your major sponsor forces you to allow Ace Reporter Girl to shadow you for a month?"

"That's one part of my life." He slid his arms around her waist, pulled her close.

For Caitlin, the feel of his lean body and strong muscles was both thrill and comfort. "There's another part?"

"The part where I want a family. Children. I've been on my own a long time. Alone. When you were at my condo for the photo shoot, it seemed so natural to have you there. To share a meal and good wine with a woman I love."

The weight on Caitlin's chest released in a flood, poured out of her...until tears stung her eyes.

"Don't cry." Rafael used a thumb to brush away the single tear that rolled down one of her cheeks. "Please don't cry."

"I didn't expect to feel this way. Didn't need it, tried to

talk myself out of it." She shook her head, still disbelieving that so much had changed in her life in so short a time. "I fought so hard against my feelings for you because I'd made one terrible mistake with my ex and I'd vowed never to make another. But how could I not fall in love with a man who has such a tender heart?"

His mouth slowly curved. "You love me?"

"Totally. You're caring and loyal. You don't strut your power or demand gratitude. You just stay in the background and do what needs to be done."

Using a fingertip, he traced the outline of her jaw. "You make me sound like a good catch."

"You're an amazing catch. Super driver, super guy, all rolled into one. Any woman would count herself lucky to have you."

"Only one does." He lifted her hand, pressed his lips against her knuckles and made her heartbeat skitter. "We can build a good life together, Caitlin. For ourselves. Our children." He turned her hand over, kissed her wrist where her pulse pounded. "Say yes," he asked her. "Please tell me you want those things, too."

"Yes. Yes, to everything."

He kissed her temple. "It seems we have some celebrating to do. And planning."

She gazed up at him through her lashes. "Which do you want to do first?"

He nuzzled her throat. "Celebrate."

"Your win at the track today?" she murmured while aching desire pooled deep inside her belly.

"My *biggest* win of the day," he said, sweeping her up into his arms. "You, Ace Reporter Girl," he added before his lips settled on hers.

* * * * *

HARLEQUIN®

A *Romance*

FOR EVERY MOOD™

Spotlight on

Heart & Home

Heartwarming romances
where love can happen
right when you least expect it.

See the next page to enjoy a sneak peek
from Harlequin Superromance®,
a Heart and Home series.

Police chief Juliette Tremblant recognized the shape of the man strolling down the street—in as calm and leisurely fashion as if it were the middle of the day rather than midnight. She slowed her car, convinced her eyes were playing tricks on her. It had been a long time since Tyler O'Neill had been seen in this town.

As she pulled to a stop at the curb, he turned toward her, and her heart about stopped.

"What the hell are you doing here, Tyler?"

"Well, if it isn't Juliette Tremblant." He made his way over to her, then leaned down so he could look her in the eye. He was close enough to touch.

Juliette was not, repeat, *not* going to touch Tyler O'Neill. Not with her fingers. Not with a ten-foot pole. There would be no touching. Which was too bad, since it was the only way she was ever going to convince herself the man standing in front of her—as rumpled and heart-stoppingly handsome now as he'd been at sixteen—was real.

And not a figment of all her furious revenge dreams.

"What are you doing back in Bonne Terre?" she asked.

"The manor is sitting empty," Tyler said and shrugged, as though his arriving out of the blue after ten years was casual. "Seems like someone should be watching over the family home."

"You?" She laughed at the very notion of him being here for any unselfish reason. "Please."

He stared at her for a second, then smiled. Her heart fluttered against her chest—a small mechanical bird powered by that smile.

"You're right." But that cryptic comment was all he offered.

Juliette bit her lip against the other questions.

Why did you go?

Why didn't you write? Call?

What did I do?

But what would be the point? Ten years of silence were all the answer she really needed.

She had sworn off feeling anything for this man long ago. Yet one look at him and all the old hurt and rage resurfaced as though they'd been waiting for the chance. That made her mad.

She put the car in gear, determined not to waste another minute thinking about Tyler O'Neill. "Have a good night, Tyler," she said, liking all the cool "go screw yourself" she managed to fit into those words.

It seems Juliette has an old score to settle with Tyler.
Pick up TYLER O'NEILL'S REDEMPTION
to see how he makes it up to her.
Available September 2010,
only from Harlequin Superromance.

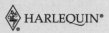

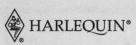

Love Inspired ®

Fan Favorite

Janet Tronstad

brings readers a heartwarming story
of love and hope with

Dr. Right

Treasure Creek, Alaska, has only one pediatrician:
the very handsome, very eligible Dr. Alex Haven.
With his contract coming to an end, he plans
to return home to Los Angeles. But Nurse
Maryann Jenner is determined to keep Alex
in Alaska, and when a little boy's life—and
Maryann's hope—is jeopardized, Alex may
find a reason to stay forever.

ALASKAN *Bride* RUSH

Available September wherever books are sold.

Steeple
Hill ®

www.SteepleHill.com